GW01066166

A BOOK CALLED HIRAETH

A Book Called Hiraeth
Longing for Wales

Compiled by

Dora Polk

ALUN BOOKS
3, Crown Street, Port Talbot, West Glamorgan

First Impression - March 1982

ISBN 0 907117 09 0

Commentary © Dora Polk 1982

Printed by :
J. D. Lewis and Sons Ltd., Gomer Press, Llandysul, Dyfed.

In memory of my father, Arthur Edward Beale of Pontnewydd, Gwent, and for my mother, born Margaret Jones, Cwmbrân, Gwent.

ACKNOWLEDGEMENTS

I am grateful to the following friends and associates for help in preparing this book :

Roland Mathias, for invaluable encouragement and practical guidance ;

Joan Bellamy Melman, for suggestions for a number of selections, and for assistance in the early stages of research ;

Gwynn ap Gwilym, for suggestions and translations of a number of appropriate quotations from the Welsh ;

Gwen Watts Jones, for advice and translation, particularly of the hymns she still sings with the congregation of the Welsh Church, Los Angeles, California ;

Cecil Price, Ceinwen Price, Gwerfyl Pierce Jones, Afan ab Alun and Lynn Hughes for suggestions and interest ;

Vera Hickman, for assistance in the final stages of compilation ;

Sally Roberts Jones, for her unique combination of editorial, creative and publishing skills ;

West Glamorgan County Library, J. V. Hughes, Local Studies Librarian, and Peter Knowles for advice and assistance in locating and preparing the illustrations.

Some of the research for this project was made possible by the award of released time allocated by California State University at Long Beach, California ; and by the award of a summer stipend for study in Wales granted by the Foundation of that University. Such practical support is greatly valued.

Special appreciation is due to all the writers out of whose work this book is woven. Specific acknowledgement of the source is made at the end of each item or extract, and fuller details of credits and attributions are given at the end of the book, while we also make grateful acknowledgement for permission to quote from the works listed.

ILLUSTRATIONS

CONTENTS

I THE NATURE OF HIRAETH

Hiraeth is the word of a thousand footnotes. Virtually untranslatable, this Welsh word has often been rendered as "longing" or "homesickness", with a caution at the bottom of the page about the inadequacy of these English equivalents. Sometimes the Welsh word is kept in the English translation with the footnote explaining this preference.

"Untranslatable" doesn't have to mean "incomprehensible". The sense of a term may be grasped through its context. The rich connotations of *hiraeth* (pronounced he-rye-th) can be conveyed through a variety of examples. Instead of taking the mystery out of the word, this invites the initiate into its mystery.

There is no shortage of material for this purpose. So powerful and complex an emotion is *hiraeth*, it has naturally become a major theme in the literature of Wales. This selection of Welsh and Anglo-Welsh work represents a fraction of what has been written on the subject.

The fountainhead of the literature of *hiraeth* lies in Wales's ancient elegies and lamentations, as revealed in a number of renderings from the Welsh in this collection. But the farther the theme travels from the source, the wider, deeper and stronger the flow becomes. *Hiraeth* has been given poetic expression more in recent times than it ever has.

It may seem contradictory that this most Welsh of emotions has found increasing expression in English over the past few centuries. But *hiraeth* is the emotion of separation, so perhaps it should be expected that Welsh exiles dispersed across the English-speaking world would pour out their feelings in the language forced on them by circumstance. *Gorau Cymro, Cymro oddi cartref*—the best Welshman is the Welshman away from home—says the old proverb, and there have been a lot of Welshmen away from home through the history of our small race, as this book will show.

While this anthology is intended to reveal our Welsh *hiraeth* to non-Welshmen, it may paradoxically be enjoyed by us Welsh ourselves, whether we live at home or abroad. Perhaps it may even serve to reinforce the ethnic bonds between the stayers and the goers, and nurture a fresh interest in our common roots among people of Welsh heritage throughout the world. There is a *hiraeth* for old songs, poems and reminiscences, too, and many included here will both stir and assuage the *hiraeth* in us for loved-and-lost, but not forgotten, people and times.

Among the best-loved utterances of *hiraeth* are these stanzas sung to the harp throughout the centuries. The intensity of the emotion comes through even in translation, differentiating it widely from mere sentimental nostalgia.

1.   HIRAETH

Tell me, men with wisdom gifted,
How hath *hiraeth* been created?
Of what stuff hath it been made,
That it doth not wear or fade?

Gold and silver wear away,
Velvet too, and silk they say;
Weareth every costly raiment:
But *hiraeth* is a lasting garment.

Now a great and cruel *hiraeth*
In my heart all day endureth,
And when I sleep most heavily,
Hiraeth comes and wakens me.

Hiraeth, hiraeth, O! depart!
Why dost thou press upon my heart?
O! move along to the bed side,
And let me rest till morning tide.

Traditional harp stanzas, translated from
the Welsh by Aneirin Talfan Davies.

Dwedwch fawrion o wybodaeth,
O ba beth y gwnaethpwyd hiraeth;
A pha ddefnydd a roid ynddo
Na ddarfyddai wrth ei wisgo.

Derfydd aur, a derfydd arian,
Derfydd melfed, derfydd sidan,
Derfydd pob dilledyn helaeth;
Eto er hyn ni dderfydd hiraeth.

Hiraeth mawr a hiraeth creulon
Sy bob dydd yn torri 'nghalon,
Pan fwyf dryma'r nos yn cysgu
Fe ddaw hiraeth, ac fe'm deffry.

Hiraeth, hiraeth, cilia, cilia,
Paid a phwyso mor drwm arna',
Nesa dipyn at yr erchwyn,
Gad i mi gael cysgu gronyn.

By contrast, the song that Harry Secombe made famous gives *hiraeth* only the force of conventional homesickness. Still, so rarely does a Welsh word find its way into the English lexicon, the popularisation of the term is significant.

2.   WE'LL KEEP A WELCOME

Verse :   Far away a voice is calling
Bells of mem'ry chime
"Come home again, come home again,"
They call through the oceans of time,—

Refrain :   We'll keep a welcome in the hillsides,
We'll keep a welcome in the vales,
This land you knew will still be singing,
When you come home again to Wales.
This land of song will keep a welcome,
And with a love that never fails,
Will kiss away each hour of Hiraeth,
When you come home again to Wales.

Words by Lyn Joshua and James Harper.

The emotional range of *hiraeth* is wide. The tone is sometimes light-hearted, sometimes laden, sometimes restorative, sometimes draining—as these further short translations from the Welsh reveal.

3. Sometimes the old people go by, leaning on their sticks, and there, with caps and smokes and warmth and *hiraeth*, they remember the revelry of old.

T. Glynne Davies,
Marged,
translated by Gwynn ap Gwilym.

4. *Hiraeth* has got me between my two breasts and my two brows: it presses on my breast as if I were nurse to it.

I shall make a ship out of the oak of love, and its mast from the wood of experience, and I shall put *hiraeth* on it to sail away from wave to wave to the country of its choice.

Traditional harp stanzas,
translated by Gwynn ap Gwilym.

> Y mae hiraeth wedi 'nghael
> Rhwng fy dwyfron a'm dwy ael;
> Ar fy mron y mae yn pwyso,
> Fel pe bawn yn famaeth iddo.
>
> Mi wnaf long o dderw cariad,
> A'i mast hi o bren y profiad;
> A rhof hiraeth arni i nofio
> O don i don i'r wlad a fynno.

5. All civility is vain amusement—as is all thought,
     all social gathering;
   everything, indeed, except *hiraeth*,
   has too soon gone away from me.

> Pob mwynder ofer afiaith—pob meddwl
> pob moddol gydymaith
> a phob peth yn wir ond hiraeth
> yn gynnar iawn oddi genny yraeth.

> Translated from a Welsh englyn in a group of sixteenth-century englynion by anonymous young women in Denbighshire.

Why are "longing" and "yearning" inadequate translations for *hiraeth*? As many another Welsh person before and after him, John Owen of Morfa Nefyn tries to analyse the complex feeling, though not necessarily definitively:

6.   We shall begin by asking: what is *hiraeth*? We have all experienced it, but maybe we have never asked what it is. This is what I believe *hiraeth* is: a sense of loss for something which a man once possessed, but is his no more. That is the difference between *hiraeth* and other things which are similar to it, between *hiraeth* and desire or yearning. A man may desire something he has never had, and yearn for something he has no experience of possessing. A man who has never had ten pounds to his name may desire to become a millionaire. A man who was brought up in a small, plain cottage and whose cradle was rocked on an earthen floor between bare walls may yearn to live in a palace amidst splendid and expensive furniture. He has no experience of such a thing, but he may yearn for it . . . But these things are not *hiraeth*. There can be no *hiraeth* except where there has been loss.

John Owen, Morfa Nefyn, from a
sermon: 'Hiraeth am Dduw'.
Translated by Gwynn ap Gwilym.

III

HIRAETH FOR PLACE :
FOR HEARTH AND VILLAGE

What are the losses which cause *hiraeth*? Most often, of course, it is the home itself that is missed—the family hearth, the homestead.

7. For many nights I had been longing for the quiet of my own bedchamber in Tŷ Nant . . . so one morning . . . I ventured to say—
    ' I think I will go down to Tŷ Nant to sleep tonight, you will not mind, will you?' . . .
    ' You mean for you to leave me there alone?' she said.
    ' Just for a night or two,' I said in a pleading voice, ' . . . I will come back . . . but now it's a silly *hiraeth* has come over me to be with . . . well, a silly *hiraeth*, that's all !'

Grace Roberts,
Lowri.

8. When I was at home, my chief pleasure was to carve,
    Whittling and whittling at my father's snug hearth,
    While my sister knitted stockings, and my mother with her flax
    Kept spinning and spinning on the floor's spotless flags.
    Lure me what may, it is my natural way
    To fly, growing blithe, on the wings of *hiraeth*,
    Towards the old home, clean, modest and warm, the best in the land.

From the Welsh of John Ceiriog Hughes (1832-87).

> Pan oeddwn i gartref fy mhenaf fwynhad
> Oedd naddu a naddu ar aelwyd glyd fy nhad :
> Tra'm chwaer efo 'i hosan a mam efo carth,
> Yn nyddu yn nyddu ar garreg lân y barth
>   Dened a ddeno, anian dynn yno,
>   Hedaf yn fy afiaeth ar adenydd hiraeth
> I'r hen dŷ, glangynes dirodres adewais yn fy ngwlad.

John Ceiriog Hughes,
Bugail yr Hafod.

The concept of "home" (*tref*) includes more than the hearth of the kin (*cartref*), or the old homestead (*hendref*). Depending on the degree of removal, the separated one may also pine for home village (*pentref*), home town (*tref*), or the larger locality (*cantref*), and no amount of advancement in distant places can compensate for such forms of *hiraeth*.

9. When I was a small boy I did not comprehend that some day I would have to leave Penygongl for ever . . . But when a house became vacant in Tai'r Efail Row it was natural that my father should take it, and move from Brynafon to live permanently at Penycaerau.

And that is where and when the harsh, cruel *hiraeth* began . .

After we had settled down at Tai'r Efail everybody was very kind to us, but to me nothing was the same any more. The road to Rhoshirwaun school was endless. The chapel wasn't the same as Nain's ; it was colder somehow and neither Huw Bryn nor William Jones, Dre Bach, sat with the elders. And when I went to fetch milk from Cadlan I had to pass two gaggles of geese—one at Tŷ Hywel and the other at Cadlan itself—and the ganders in both gaggles had taken a dislike to me—of that I am sure. They were much more fierce than the geese of Rhent. And I missed running down to Caerodyn for butter. Worse than all these things, however, was the continuous feeling that Penygongl was so terribly far away.

J. G. Williams,
Pigau'r Sêr,
translated by Gwynn ap Gwilym.

10. HIRAETH AM FEIRION (Longing for Merioneth)

Would that the mountain that hides Merioneth
    were under the sea—
If only I could see it again before my trembling heart breaks.

Translated from a Welsh folk verse
for the harp.

11.   It is quite true what you say about one getting accustomed even to these periodic separations from one's family—but all the same I get spasms of *hiraeth*. You know very well that the pressure to bring us together invariably comes from me. I have led a very strenuous and anxious life for the past five years . . . but I always come back with a sensation of restful delight to Brynawelon. I only wish I could get such a fortnight there as I enjoyed immediately after my election collapse. In spite of my complete physical prostration I never enjoyed my life as I did then. I felt perfectly happy. It is such a fortnight as that I want now to set me up for the Session.

Excerpt from a letter by David
Lloyd George (1863-1945) written
in February 1896.

12.   This morning, as I walked in the sunshine with the slow unsteady steps of age among the dear familiar environs of Pen-y-bryn, I looked up at the old grey house which has been the abiding-place of my forbears for so many generations. Here every stick and stone holds something of their lives, as they hold mine, but soon, alas, strangers will break upon the sweet continuance of the centuries, for I am now the last of the long line. There are those who deem it strange, though why I do not know, that I should have spent the whole of my long life in this small compass in Llanara, the little *pentre* on the upper slopes of the sweet and lovely valley of the Clwyd. Before I became too old and infirm for journeyings, often I paid visits to Rhyl and Llandudno, fair places by the sea, and to cities like Liverpool and Chester, but so strong was my *hiraeth* for Dyffryn Clwyd that always I returned before the end of my intended stay, for there was nowhere else for me, then as now, nowhere but the hills and moors of home, and the little *nant*, which has sung its way through my life from the days when its music mingled with my mother's lullabies, as she rocked my wooden cradle in the hearthplace. All along the ages has this vale been sung by bards and minstrels as being the fairest in Wales: indeed, Taid often used to tell of a famous divine from South Wales, who when he rounded the bend of the Bwlch on horseback from the shire of Flint, and for the first time, beheld Dyffryn Clwyd stretching in all

its summer beauty to the sea, was so overcome that he knelt by the roadside and with tears in his eyes, exclaimed ' Well done, God ! ! !' And no wonder that the old preacher felt such deep emotion at the sight, for to the east rise Moel Fammau, Moel Fenlli and the hill of Bedd y Cawr, the last and ancient resting-place of the giant chieftain lying there so calm and serene through the turmoil of the ages. To the west the uplands rise gently to the great peaty moors of Hiraethog where it is said that the fairies, the Tylwyth Teg, still dance in their magic rings o' nights, and hobgoblins haunt the dark eerie wastes.

From the summit of old Moel Fammau with its square stone tower, a landmark even in the English border shires, can be seen on a clear summer's day the busy waters of the Mersey, and the masts of great sailing ships in the river Dee; sometimes, like a faint smudge on the Irish Sea, the Isle of Man shows itself. Looking nearer, the eye falls on the shires of Flint and Arvon with Snowdon's peak rising in proud challenge to the sky. But soft and gentle are the hills of the Clwyd, not harsh and frightening like the rocky crags of Arvon; there they stand like great blue walls, sheltering the people of the valley from the noisy world beyond, and it is glad I am that when my time comes, as come it will soon, I shall die as I have lived beneath their shadow.

Grace Roberts,
Lowri.

13.   In the silence of forests where flowers come of age and the prettiest birds on earth make their home in the trees, my heart flies to Glamorgan where there are furnaces, smoke and industry, where crowds of men give expression to their needs . . . County of mighty rebels, county of agony and great oppression, county of prophets who turn their faces through the smoke towards the dawn ; in my dreams my heart encamps within it; *hiraeth* for my dear Glamorgan fills my soul.

T. E. Nicholas (1879-1971),
from *Hiraeth am Forgannwg*,
translated by Gwynn ap Gwilym.

IV   HIRAETH FOR THE HOMELAND : FOR WALES'S SACRED SOIL AND BEAUTY

The most painful form of *hiraeth* for place is created when separation is from the homeland itself. The Welshman is bound to Mam Cymru by bands of unbreakable loyalty, as the national anthem expresses:

> Gwlad, gwlad, pleidiol wyf i'm gwlad;
> Tra môr yn fur i'r bur hoff bau,
> O bydded i'r hen iaith barhau.
>
> Ieuan ap Iago—Evan James,
> (1809-1878)

Literally translated, this reads:

> Country, country, upholding am I of my country;
> While the sea is a wall to the pure fond soil,
> O may the old language continue.

Of the many translations, one of the freer versions has enjoyed considerable popularity among the Anglo-Welsh, perhaps because it brings in a missing reference to *hiraeth:*

> Wales, Wales, my mother's sweet home is in Wales;
> Till death be pass'd my love shall last,
> My longing, my *hiraeth* for Wales.
>
> Translated by Eben Fardd and
> Owain Alaw.

The concept of the beloved country includes a belief in the sacredness of the soil, which is reinforced by the extraordinary natural beauty of the Welsh landscape. The green mountains, woods and valleys of Cymru are sorely missed by most expatriates, and their memory is a perpetual source of *hiraeth*.

Mountain rill, that darkling, sparkling,
Winds and wanders down the hill,
'Mid the rushes, whispering, murmuring,
Oh that I were like the rill!

Mountain ling, whose flower and fragrance
Sorest longing to me bring
To be ever on the mountains—
Oh that I were like the ling!

Mountain bird, whose joyous singing
On the wholesome breeze is heard,
Flitting hither, flitting thither—
Oh that I were like the bird!

Mountain child am I, and lonely
Far from home my song I sing;
But my heart is on the mountain
With the birds amid the ling.

John Ceiriog Hughes (18328-187),
Nant y Mynydd,
translated by Edmund O. Jones.

Nant y Mynydd groyw, loyw,
Yn ymdroelli tua'r pant,
Rhwng y brwyn yn sisial ganu—
O na bawn i fel y nant!

Grug y Mynydd yn eu blodau,
Edrych arnynt hiraeth ddug
Am gael aros ar y bryniau
Yn yr awel efo'r grug.

Adar mân y mynydd uchel
Godant yn yr awel iach,
O'r naill drum i'r llall yn 'hedeg,—
O na bawn fel 'deryn bach!

Mab y Mynydd ydwyf innau
Oddi cartref yn gwneud cân,
Ond mae 'nghalon yn y mynydd
Efo'r grug a'r adar mân.

Dear motherland, forgive me, if too long
I hold the halting tribute of my song;
Letting my wayward fancy idly roam
Far, far from thee, my early home.
There are some things too near,
Too infinitely dear
For speech; the old ancestral hearth,
The hills, the vales that saw our birth,
Are hallowed deep within the reverent breast:
And who of these keeps silence, he is best.

Yet would not I appear
Who have known many a brighter land and sea
Since first my boyish footsteps went from thee,
The less to hold thee dear;
Or lose in newer beauties the immense
First love for thee, O birth-land, which fulfils
My inmost heart and soul,—
Love for thy smiling and sequestered vales,
Love for thy winding streams which sparkling roll
Through thy rich fields, dear Wales,
From long perspectives of thy folded hills.

Ay! these are sacred, all;
I cannot sing of them, too near they are.
What if from out thy dark yews, gazing far,
I sat and sang, Llangunnor! of the vale
Through which fair Towy winds her lingering fall,
Gliding by Dynevor's wood-crowned steep,
And, alternating swift with deep,
By park and tower a living thing
Of loveliness meandering;
And traced her flowing onward still,
By Grongar dear to rhyme, or Dryslwyn's castled hill
Till the fresh upward tides prevail,
Which stay her stream and bring the sea-borne sail,
And the broad river roll majestic down
Beneath the gray walls of my native town.

Would not my fancy quickly stray
To thee, sea-girt St. David's, far away,
A minster on the deep; or, further still,
To you, grand mountains, which the stranger knows:
Eryri throned amid the clouds and snows,
The dark lakes, the wild passes of the north;
Or Cader, a stern sentinel looking forth
Over the boisterous main; or thee, dear Isle
Not lovely, yet which canst my thought beguile—
Mona, from whose fresh wind-swept pastures came
My grandsire, bard and patriot, like in name
Whose verse his countrymen still love to sing
At bidding-feast or rustic junketing? . . .

I may not sing of you,
Or tell my love—others there are who will,
Who haply bear not yet a love so true
As that my soul doth fill—
If to applaud it lead, or gain, or fame;
Better than this it were to bear the pain
Which comes to higher spirits when they know
They fire in other souls no answering glow;
Love those who love me not again,
And leave my country naught, not even a name.

Sir Lewis Morris, (1833-1907).

16.   They were delayed in the King's household some time, on
account of the charter not being completed. Gladys began
to grow weary of the gay scene, she longed to be where her
heart was, in Cambria, surrounded by her people, she grew
impatient to stand upon the battlements of Harlech once
more; . . . She longed to stand again knee deep among
the purple heather of her native hill sides, to listen to the
browsing of the deer and the bleating of the sheep, the dashing
of the cataracts or the roaring of the wind as it lifts the foam
crested waves and dashes them into spray among the rocks;
she longed again to rest her eyes from the place of her repose
upon the deep blue waters of her native bay.

Anne Beale (1816-1900),
Gladys of Harlech.

HEAD IN THE CLOUDS

Head in the clouds to you is a worn phrase
Weakly used to indicate disapproval
Of somebody else's ability to evade
Or ignore the day's burden and trial.

But to us who were born above Pencarreg
Head in the clouds is true, is simply true.
Nor all the brazen comfort of the sun
Can dissipate the clouds upon Penrhiw.

And if you say, as other friends have said,
That I walk always with my head in a cloud,
I am wilful enough to take you literally
And let your saying make me homesick and proud.

Homesick for clouded hills that never lose
The loom and shape they had when I,
My head in other clouds, trod their old paths
Too proud then to know that I too would die.

Proud now to know that when I have to die
My head has always been in clouds: first those
That still hang low over Pencarreg and Penrhiw,
And then the ones in which you shroud me close.

                              T. Harri Jones (1921-1965).

LINES

Behind the Mournes the sunrise like a flower
Deep-hearted scatters blushing petals, so
The sea below is now a rosy glow,
Yet all the glory passes with the hour.
But Oh! in Wales the ragged mountains wait
Eternal, bathed by dawn-flush more divine.
The shadow is as loving as the shine
And every mountain-pass is heaven's gate.
Lough Kernon surely is a passing dream:

It steals my heart a moment, but its spell
Is swiftly broken. Oh, the pungent smell
Of thyme above the Morfa, and the gleam,
The cold green gleam of Tecwyn in the mist
Hold me a slave for ever. Sunset-kissed
The waves at Garreg Goch are all my dream.
I still can see the curlews on the shore
At Morfa Bychan wheel towards the sea;
And every plashing wavelet sing to me
Of Cantre'r Gwaelod's mystic faery lore.
The mists of Wales are clinging round my heart,
The hills of Wales will never let me be.
I hear them calling o'er the restless sea,
And at their phantom bidding I depart.

G. H. Roberts.

19.   In his punishment cell Myrddin Tomos could envisage the
lush, nourishing meadows on the banks of the Tywi, the rich
harvests, the abounding hills, and the moors which were as
smooth and even as lawns. The sun yellowed the wheat,
ripened the barley and the oats. The cows meditated standing up to their udders in the grass. In the dairies the pots
were full of cream and the brass pans of whey. Printed
pounds of butter lay in the keeler, and whey dripped from
the cheese vessels under the *wring*. Eggs stood on top of
each other in the pans, white eggs and brown eggs, and the
big, blue-white eggs of the ducks. Carmarthenshire seemed
to Myrddin Tomos's eyes a land overflowing with milk and
porridge . . . A living desire would return to his heart and a
hiraeth to see the land of his youth. He saw himself again
walking with his friends along the paths of Llansadwrn,
but they could not know the happiness of feet which had
been fettered, or the blessing of sun and breeze to a mind
which had been on the verge of madness. He would go again
to fetch the cows for milking, and would see them on a misty
morning like huge, magic beings, or would watch on a frosty
morning the breath coming out of their nostrils like steam
from the spout of a kettle. He would take care lest the cow
in calf should slip on the slope. He would follow the team
of horses between the plough-handles, and, after a day's

26

ploughing, free the horses from their chains at the furrow's end and fondle their steaming necks. He would once again hold a fork and a pitchfork, smell in his nostrils the smells of work and sweat, drink milk-and-butter in the heat of the harvest, and hear the cross-cut saw, on a rainy day, singing in the clefts of the fire-wood in the cart-house. He would plant his fork in the dung-heap and pull the manure apart, would lift a forkful of it, alive with earthworms and yellow gadflies and would take it, load after load, to the field. He would spread heaps of manure all over the field and then scatter the big, warm, brown lumps. He imagined himself strolling over the meadows and the mountains with all his senses alive and hungry. His eyes would be intoxicated by the colours and the pictures, and his ears could not hear enough of the noises and sounds. He would lie flat on his belly on the earth and suck into his nostrils every smell, the smell of hay and flowers, thyme and mint, the smell of wheat and vegetables and the dung of animals.

When the *hiraeth* for the land of his birth came over him, he would take the three-legged stool in his cell, place it under the window and climb onto it so that he could direct his gaze through the bars towards Carmarthenshire and drink into his soul from afar the vigour of its streams.

(N.B. Myrddin Tomos was a conscientious objector in World War I).

D. Gwenallt Jones (1899-1968),
Plasau'r Brenin,
translated by Gwynn ap Gwilym.

20.   There is a spirit of Wales which is unconfined to word and language: in Nature "day unto day uttereth speech," and the morning stars sing sweetly together for all to hear in the valleys of the west, where dawn rises slow out of England— an England still strange and far and cold to Welshmen's hearts. Love of their lovely home is the tie that binds all Welshmen in its spell, the beauty and sorrow of Nature breathes through the old Welsh tunes that all can understand. "Annwyl Gymru, gwlad y Gân" (Dear Wales, the land of song) is more than a slogan for Eisteddfod week; it is a true statement of feeling . . .

Today, perhaps, it is the naked whalebacks of the hills and the tumbled mountain precipices which lure the wanderer's imagination, but surely those who know this Wales have each their images engraven in the mind, some skyline shape that haunts them in their dreams, some view of sea or shore they linger on . . .

Eiluned and Peter Lewis,
The Land of Wales.

V HIRAETH FOR THE WELSH LANGUAGE

Love of Wales is inextricably bound up with the Welsh
language. Welsh-speaking exiles, scattered across the English-
speaking world, suffer constant *hiraeth* for their mother tongue.

21.   FROM EXILE

> It's bright the icy foam as it flows,
> It's fierce in January great sea tumult,
> It's woe's me the language, long-wished-for speech
> For the sake of tales, would be sweet to my ear.
>
> Ability in English I never had,
> Neither knew phrases of passionate French:
> A stranger and foolish, when I've asked questions
> It turned out crooked—I spoke North Welsh!
>
> On a wave may God's son grant us our wish
> And out from amongst them readily bring us
> To a Wales made one, contented and fair,
> To a prince throned, laden nobly with gifts,
> To the lord of Dinorwig's bright citadel land,
> To the country of Dafydd, where Welsh freely flows!

> Dafydd Benfras (13th century),
> translated by Anthony Conran.

22.   Where I played of old are men who knew me not ; a
friend or two may remember me, scarce two where once
were a hundred. I am a man cut off, obscure, an exile from
Môn, a stranger to our ancient tongue, strong-syllabled, a
stranger to the sweet strains of the Muse. Full of care I am,
ah me to speak of it! And full of longing, sunk in heavy-
hearted sorrow.

> Goronwy Owen (1723-1769),
> from *Hiraeth am Fôn* (Longing for Anglesey),
> translated by H. Idris Bell.

23.   There are three things a Welshman must think about when emigrating, his country, his language and his religion. He must be determined to give up many comforts and to be strong.

Letter from T. R. Evans in Plymouth,
Carroll County, Missouri,
Alan Conway, *The Welsh in America.*

Even the Anglo-Welsh—those deprived of the native tongue by anglicisation—pine for the music of Welsh and the Anglo-Welsh dialect when away from home.

24.   Those first months in the autumn of 1942, I loathed the fogs, London's apparent offhandedness. I longed for the provincial friendliness of Welsh people. I wanted to hear a bit of Welsh spoken, or, at least, the accented sing-song voices that I knew so well with all their cosmic portentousness. At King's College I joined the Welsh Society and even gave a talk on Welsh poetry. I chanted William Barnes's translation of an anonymous ninth-century Welsh lament until tears of home-sickness came into my eyes:

Cynddylan's hall is all in gloom tonight;
No fire, no lighted room:
Amid the stillness of the tomb . . .

Dannie Abse,
A Poet in the Family.

VI HIRAETH FOR WELSH CULTURAL INSTITUTIONS AND VALUES

Hiraeth, too, is felt for the institutions of the homeland, cultural and religious, and pride in those institutions endures from generation to generation in emigrant Welsh families.

25. The Welsh people in the neighbourhood have enjoyed fairly good health this year . . . My mother has enjoyed good health throughout except that she had a touch of ague last October; at times too, she yearns for the religious meetings of Wales.

> Postscript from William G. Bebb
> to his uncle, October 10th, 1850,
> Alan Conway, *The Welsh in America.*

26. TO THE POETRY SOCIETIES IN WALES (I GYM-DEITHASAU'R BEIRDD YNG NGHYMRU)

Often from America I think of Clwb Gwerin Cefni,
Of the Class in Talgarreg or the Poets of Dyfi.
They are the impossible, and it would be foolish to believe, in our own
Twentieth century, that the family, although denied its freedom, can keep its heart.
Often through the winter in Quebec, seeing some mornings the frost
That grew inside the trees, through their branches, and the few
Blanch apples that ripened overnight—white nights, white nights—
I cannot but meditate on the talk of craft and basic principles
In fruitful village halls, till the early hours, in the nooks
And crannies of Wales, on the poets in the deep belly of the country whom I will praise a thousand times to my friends,
That they still sharpen the blades of their ears, an incredible peasantry.

31

To them will come one from Llanddowror and another from
  Bro Gynin
To taste their homely dishes. The treetrunk is still so solid
That the branches can but continue to throw out their over-
  flowing plums.
More clearly than the springs of Wales, I remember her
  poets.
They scratch at my hiraeth oftener than her hills. There
  isn't over there one river
That has carved its banks more deeply through my middle
  than the carvers of poems—
White nights, white nights—on the banks of Dyfi and the
  banks of Cefni.
America does not know—and what land in Europe knows—
  of the duelling
(Nor its reason) among farmers, garage-hands, postmen,
  ministers.
As I write their names in the snow, I know the warmth of
  their company
As though I cut their memory in the icy wind of time—
  Dyfi, Talgarreg and Cefni.

Bobi Jones,
translated by R. Gerallt Jones

(N.B. Clwb Gwerin Cefni is an informal literary society and discussion group
in Llangefni, Anglesey; it comprises men from a vast variety of backgrounds and
following a diversity of callings; it is one of many such literary groups in rural
Wales. Such were Waldo's class at Talgarreg and the poets at Llanbrynmair,
Bro Dyfi.)

27.   On 19 July we left about two o'clock in the morning and
were towed by a steamboat until she could sail herself; and
here we were on the open sea for the first time in our lives,
leaving the dear land of our birth . . . What was the strangest
thing for me on the voyage was spending Sunday. I remembered every minute of the Sabbath in Cwmbach, the sermons,
the singing, the praying, and the Sunday School, but on
Sunday 3 August I was heavy at heart; it was the third
Sunday for me without a religious service.

Letter from William Jenkins
to J. Morgans, Cwmbach,
Alan Conway, *The Welsh in America.*

Nant-y-Glo, Abertillery, Gwent.

Paxton's Tower, Vale of Tywi, Dyfed.

28.   It is the fashion of certain critics to speak of Wales as small
and obscure, without great men, with a language which is a
semi-barbarous jargon. Those who talk thus are ignorant
of the very alphabet of human history . . . Wales an obscure
country! Why she is the mother of British civilisation . . .
she gave birth to that spirit of civil and religious liberty which
is the proudest boast of England today. In her bosom was
nourished that vital principle of equity and justice which
has permeated the soul of modern political institutions . . .
Wales an obscure country! Every foot of her soil is classic,
every valley and glen and mountain top is hallowed by
glorious memories. Her Cromlechs, her Druidical remains,
and her monuments of Roman possession attest the grandeur
of her past . . .

Are you aware that America—land of our love, land of our
adoption—was first discovered by Welshmen; that ages
before Columbus landed on San Salvador, Prince Madoc
and his expedition of hardy Cymry had crossed the stormy
ocean and planted their conquering banners on these western
shores? And although the issue was disastrous, a remnant
of his followers survived, penetrated to the heart of this continent, founded a colony, and through centuries of evil
fortune preserved something of their native characteristics,
their native faith and language. Succumbing to pestilence,
they have disappeared from the face of the earth, but the
memory of the "Welsh Indians" will ever be dear to the
student of history.

> From a report of the speech of Samuel
> Williams, President of the Mutual
> Aid Society of San Francisco, on St.
> David's Day, 1871.

Love of Wales is also embodied in a wealth of detail—beloved
objects, emblems, songs and customs. They both create and
assuage *hiraeth*, especially on St. David's Day, *Gŵyl Ddewi*,
Wales's national festival, the *Gŵyl mabsant*, the feast of her Patron
Saint.

29.   . . . The first of March, there is such a welling of *hiraeth*,
nostalgia, such a harvest of King Alfred daffodils, such a
burgeoning of leeks, such a roasting of celebratory dinners,

such a toasting at parties, such a tinkling of harps, such a flap of Red Dragons, such an ectoplasmic outpouring from BBC Wales, such a roar of *Men of Harlech*, you would think the people would suffocate from pride, or, at the very least, bring Owain Glyndwr, the medieval warrior prince and hero, . . . down from the mountain.

Trevor Fishlock,
Wales and the Welsh.

VII   THE SUFFERERS OF HIRAETH

Hiraeth for home and homeland is not exclusive to the separated state. It can be felt projectively, before leaving, at the mere prospect of separation. And it can be felt at the very moment of returning, as all the pent-up longing is released.

30.   Never had the thrush music sounded more plaintive to him than on that evening. He leaned on the stable door, looking at his mother's garden, knowing that this memory of it would have to last him a long while. What he felt has no word in English but the Welsh call it *hiraeth*. This is a sickness whose symptoms are a lump in the throat and hollowness in the stomach at the thought of separation from home and the people and places which belong. It is more than home-sickness, because it is infected with girls with dark hair and pale skin, and with music in the minor key, and mountains, and a pewter-coloured sky.

Twm's moment of *hiraeth* was seen by Catherine on her way to gather herbs and petals. She withdrew into a shadow so as not to let him know. The mother looked at her son and saw—for possibly the first time in their twenty-eight years—a man.

Lynn Hughes,
Hawkmoor.

31.   . . . He knew it had to be done sometime—this journey to her father's people up in the mountains. The Welsh were funny people—they got something out of it, this journey to the old folks at home, even if the home were a hovel. And as they all had a home somewhere, they would all have to go back to it . . .

They had come to the brow of the last hill. Below them the road dropped into a *cwm*. A torrent tumbled over the mountain into it, swilling through the heather, leaping down into a spume of silver. And there, below them, was the house, standing out of the earth, with its upblown smoke curling up to them, and the pandemonium of barking dogs and the geese shrieking. It had all suddenly come to life . . .

She reached her feet into the fender and leaned back into the old horsehair chair. The worn old house possessed her—the brass harness round about, the old dresser with its line on line of blue china plate, the rich earth smell of the peat. That fire had never been out for two hundred years, her father had always told her. And here it was! And all around, through the little tight shut windows, was the moist green of the mountain, reaching up like a shelf, and the distant rumble of the brook.

Pant-y-Pistyll—the Hollow of the Spring. Always the drifting mist, for ever lifting, and the noise of the water, the sharp high tinkle to the deep, harsh earth-flooded roar of the winter: the green earth, the smell of peat and the high blue crust of the mountain—that was her home, her father's home, and that was where she belonged. She let it all possess her, gave herself up to it, as to a lover. She had gone away from herself, far, far away. Now she was—only now she was: never before, perhaps never again, but now she was.

'Oh, *Nain*' (grandmother), she said. She threw her arms around the old woman and bent her head in the old shawl.

'There, there,' said the old woman, brushing back her hair with her old withered hands. She pressed her to her old breasts and crooned to her as to a child, taking the deep, breaking sobs to herself.

'The old *hiraeth*' (longing), she said to her son, standing beside them. The old mother waved him away. He went out into the yard.

Geraint Goodwin (1903-1941),
The White Farm.

Expatriation of any kind, however temporary and voluntary, can bring *hiraeth* to the Welshman. Many a sailor-adventurer of bye-gone days, and professional, businessman, or tourist of recent times, has suffered the emotion.

32.   I have thousands of tales to tell when I come home, but they are so long I cannot start writing them. Indeed, I should not be writing at all tonight, I am so tired. But there

has come over me a fit of *hiraeth* for Wales, not that sweet *hiraeth* which one sometimes feels, but a bitter, agonising *hiraeth*, a *hiraeth* like the *hiraeth* of Jeremiah, the prophet . . . I shall be starting back for the Rhine as soon as I get up tomorrow morning, and I hope to reach Mainz before nightfall. I shall forget my *hiraeth* when I see the Seven Mountains and the valleys of the Rhine, but you know it will always be with me.

O. M. Edwards (1858-1920),
O'r Bala i Geneva,
translated by Gwynn ap Gwilym.

33.   . . . In the old *awdl-gywydd* measure adapted to a four-line stanza is a 16th century poem of longing for home (*hiraeth*), a favourite theme of Welsh poets, written by Sir Sion Gruffydd, Chaplain to Mr. William Thomas, whilst they were in Flanders . . .

> I'm a man living, through God's power,
> a stranger to his nation;
> the cause of all my sorrowing
> is longing for Caernarvon.
>
> Dyn wy'n byw drwy nerth y Tad,
> ymhell o'i wlad yn estron
> wyf ofalus a phaham
> o hiraeth am Gaernarvon.

And so on for fourteen simple but deeply felt stanzas.

Gwyn Williams,
An Introduction to Welsh Poetry.

34.   (The poet is describing the source of the "furnishings of polar ivory" in the finery worn by Arthur's wife, "our own Gwenhwyfar":)

to obtain which

who but Manawydan himself, on the whale-path, but four and a half degrees of latitude without the arctic parallel, two hundred and twenty nautical miles south-east by south of Islont[1] with Thor's Fairy-Haven[2] Isles looming on his star-

board beam about six Gaulish leagues, alone and by himse¡
—except for his *môr-forwyn*-mates[3]—running free with the
wind on the starboard side, carried away and handsomely,
the rare dexter tooth of the living bull narwhal that bluff-
nosed the southwester nose-ender with spiralled ivories
lancing the bright spume scud.

The cruising old *wicing* !
This he averred he achieved on his ocean-trip to the Thing-
Ness in Gynt-land,[4] his *hiraeth*[5] upon him, some fifteen days
out from his *dinas* in Cemeis in Demetia[6]

(where he latins his oghams).
Plotting his course by the North Drift route that streams
him warm to Hordaland . . .

[1]Islont, iss-lont, accent on first syllable, called also Ynys-yr-Ia, Island of Snow,
Iceland.
[2]The Faeroe group.
[3]*môrforwyn*, sea-maiden, morr-vorr-win, accent on the penultimate syllable. As
has already been noted, Manawydan, man-now-ud-an, was a sea-god and perhaps
an agriculture-god, who appears in the tales as a Welsh ruler with magical powers.
[4]Thing-Ness, from thing (assembly) and ness (promontory).   It has been
suggested that there is a connection between this compound and the Welsh word
for city, *dinas*, din-ass, accent on first syllable. Gynt, ' g ' hard, from *gentes*, the
Scandinavian peoples.
[5]*hiraeth*, heer-aeth, ae as ah+eh, the Welsh word for yearning or longing, is also
found in place-names as in the Hiraethog hills in Denbighshire, and there is the
theory that connects the word with a site-name envisaged in a Welsh-Scandinavian
complex.   In his book *Mabinogi Cymru* (1930) Mr. Timothy Lewis gives a map
showing a suggested cosmology of the world of the old tales and on it ' Hiraeth ' is
identified with Hordaland, now the district of South Bergenhus in Norway.
[6]Demetia or Dyfed in South-West Wales.
Cemeis, kem-ice, accent on first syllable.
This ancient division of northern Pembrokeshire is said to be the home of much
that went to the formation of the oldest legendary deposits.

David Jones (1895-1974),
from Mabinog's Liturgy in *The Anathemata*.

35.   HIRAETH IN N.W. 3

The sight of the English is getting me down.
Fly westward, my heart, from this festering town
On the Wings of a Dove—and a First Class Return—
To the front room of ' Cartref ' at Ynys-y-Wern.

Swift through the dark flies the 5.49,
Past Slough and past Didcot and derelict mine,
Past pubs and Lucanias and adverts for ales
Till the back-sides of chapels cry ' Welcome to Wales '.

The lights of the chip-shop shine bright in the dark,
The couples lie laced in the asphalted park;
In the vestry of Carmel (conductor, Seth Hughes)
The iron-lunged Gleemen are raping the Muse.

They're ' Comrades', they're ' Martyrs', they're ' Crossing
    the Plain',
They're roaring of Love in a three-part refrain,
But what hymns from Novello's, at threepence a part,
Can mirror the music I feel in my heart?

Glorious welcome that's waiting for me,
Hymns on the harmonium, Welsh-cakes for tea,
A lecture on Marx: his importance today,
All the raptures of love from a Bangor B.A.

                                    Wynford Vaughan-Thomas.

36.   Before I came back to live in Wales, a very little time ago,
I was travelling on a morning train from Oxford to London
when, suddenly, the desire to live neither in Oxford nor in
London, or to travel between them came very near to knocking me down, which would not be difficult.

I was, at that moment, chillily perched on a stool, old
from sleep, at the tumbler-circled counter in the bellying
buffet-car . . .

There, all about me, chastely dropping, with gloved and
mincing, just-so fingers, saccharine tablets into their cups of
stewed Thameswater, or poising their cigarette-holders like
blowpipes, or daintily raising, the little finger crooked, a
currant bun to the snapping flash of their long, strong teeth,
tall and terrible women neighed: women inaccessible as
goat crags . . .

There, all about me, long thin accents with yellow waist-
coats and carefully windswept hair, one lock over the eye,
bleated and fluted. In a drawl of corduroy at the tea-urn,
vowels were plucked and trussed.

Tiny, dry, egghead dons, smelling of water-biscuit, with
finickety lips and dolls' bowties like butterflies poisoned and
pinned, solved the crossword puzzles behind their octagonal
glasses and smirked their coffee up . . .

And then and there, as I watched them all, desire raised
its little fist.
I did not want to be in England, now that they were there.
I did not want to be in England, whether they were there
or not.
I wanted to be in Wales.

Dylan Thomas (1914-1953),
from a broadcast, June 23, 1949.

37. BY THE PACIFIC

On the fair green shore of the sea of calm,
Where life to the grave its challenge throws,
Where grove on grove of the stately palm
No yellowing Autumn ever knows.

I sit, and I feel the low wind play
Across my cheek with its dreamy breath;
I see the swift night conquer the day
And the dying sunset bleed to death.

Behind me there in the distance stand
The Sierras crowned with eternal snow,
Where down broad beds of the golden sand
Unnumbered rivers exhaustless flow.

I am sick and lonely far from home;
Long have I wandered unknown ways;
But out of the past with healing come
The sweet kind thoughts of the buried days.

R. Silyn Roberts (1871-1930),
translated by H. Idris Bell.

VIII   THE HIRAETH OF MEDIAEVAL
WELSH EXILES FROM INVADERS.

When the exile has small hope of return—as has been the
case for so many of the Welsh over the centuries—the *hiraeth*
is the more bitter and unassuageable. Such was the suffering
of those Cymru (the comrades) driven from their land by
the Romans, the marauding Saxons and the Normans in the
Middle Ages.

38.

Men launched the assault, nourished as one
A year over mead, grand their design.
How sad their tale, insatiable longing,
Bitter their home, no child to cherish it.
How long the grief for them and mourning,
For ardent men of wine-nourished lands.
Gododdin's Gwlyged, warm in welcome,
Renowned Mynyddawg's feast he fashioned,
And its cost, the battle of Catraeth.

Aneirin (6th century),
from *The Gododdin*,
(A Lamentation at the loss to the English at Catraeth),
translated by Joseph P. Clancy.

Gwyr a gryssyssant buant gytvaeth.
blwydyn od uch med mawr eu haruaeth.
mor dru eu hadrawd wy. angawr hiraeth.
gwenwyn eu hadlam nyt mab mam ae maeth.
mor hir eu hetlit ac eu hetgyllaeth
en ol gwyr pebyr temyr gwinvaeth,
gwlyget gododin en erbyn fraeth.
ancwyn mynydawc enwawc e gwnaeth.
a phrit er prynu breithyell gatraeth.

41

39.

Loud are birds; gravel is wet.
Leaves fall; sad is the homeless one.
I will not deny it, I am ill tonight.

Loud are birds; wet is the shore.
Sky is bright; wide
The wave. Heart withered from longing.

Gorddyar adar; gwlyb gro.
Dail cwyddid; difryd difro.
Ni wadaf, wyf claf heno.

Gorddyar adar; gwlyb traeth.
Eglur nwyfre; ehalaeth
Ton. Gwyw calon rhag hiraeth.

*　　*　　*

Crutch of wood, constant branch,
May you support an old man full of longing—
Llywarch, the steadfast talker.

Baglan bren, gangen fodawg,
Cynhelych hen hiraethog—
Llywarch lleferydd fodawg.

Llywarch Hen (6th century),
Translated by Patrick K. Ford.

40.

Height of sword-strife, pouring forth of wine,
I am left with smile lost, aged by longing.
I lost when he fought for Pennawg's land
A valiant man, savage, sparing none.
He launched the assault past Tren, proud land.
I shall mourn till I enter steadfast earth
Cynddylan slain, famed as Caradawg.

Mawredd gyminedd, gwin waredawg,
Wyf colledig wen, hen hiraethawg.
Collais pan amwyth alaf Pennawg
Gwr dewr diachar diarbedawg.
Cyrchai drais tra Thren, tir trahawg.
Ef cwynif oni fwyf yn ddaear fodawg,
O leas Cynddylan, clod Caradawg.

Marwnad Cynddylan (Lament for Cynddylan) (6th century),
from *Songs of Llywarch Hen*,
translated by Joseph P. Clancy.

41. A LAY OF SOFTEST MELODY TO THE MEMORY OF CARACTUS.

(Caractus, or Caradawg, or Caradoc, led the Silures, natives of
Gwent against the invading Romans in the first century ; he was
vanquished and sent to Rome in chains.)

Soft notes of mourning die gently away upon mine ear.
I weep to the soft notes of mine harp, and a sadly-pleasing
anguish steals upon my soul. First known of British slaves,
valiant Caractacus ! thy name steals upon the senses . . .
O my country ! dear lost Siluria ! how art thou fallen !
Where now the simple hut, where brave Caractacus gave
audience to men of might? Where now the clay-built shed,
where sung the bards of Gwent of nought but love and
liberty? Lovers of strife, fierce haughty Romans ! Why
invade our peaceful, rude, uncultivated isle? . . . O my
forefathers ! lovers of simplicity ! but with your lives you
lost your liberty. Curst be the foe, who fought for nought
but strife; and immortal be the name of Caractacus !

Lay the Third of the Lays of Caruth.
from the collection of Anne Elfe.

42 GRIFFITH, SON OF CYNAN

(Gruffyth ab Cynan's betrayal and imprisonment by the
Normans at the end of the 11th century is here lamented.)

Longing for my beloved land
Is a cruel knot in my heart,
But the villain who counselled treachery
Has high honour for his part;

By night and day I sorrow here,
Bound, in the midst of the foe;
If only I were in Gwalia free
Where the hidden valleys go!

I long for every hill and vale,
Moor, meadow and mountain tall,
Yearning for my lost wife and babes
Strikes through my fainting soul;
Honour, respect and majesty
I once from my followers gained;
They fled, and nothing is left to me
But this prison where I am chained.

Talhaiarn, (John Jones, 1810-1869),
translated by S. Jones.

Mae hiraeth am fy annwyl wlad
Yn gwlwm am fy nghalon i,
Mae'r adyn a gynlluniodd frâd
Yn uchel yn ei rwysg a'i fri;
A minau'n cwyno nos a dydd,
Yn rhwym ym mysg gelynol lu;
Ow ! Ow ! na fawn yn Ngwalia rydd,
Yn rhodio ei dyffrynoedd cu.

Mae hiraeth am bob bryn a phant,
A gwaen a dôl, a mynydd ban,
A hiraeth am fy ngwraig a mhlant,
Yn treiddio drwy fy nghalon wan;
Anrhydedd, mawredd, parch, a bri
A gefais gynt gan ddeiliaid pur;
Maent wedi ffoi nid oes i mi
Ond carchar a chadwynau dur.

43. OVER THE ROCK

Over the rock afar I roam
Sadly I leave my mountain home.
Deep my sorrow.
Dark the morrow
When I cross the ocean foam.

Cold in hate, the tyrant's hand
Binds his fetters o'er the land,
Vain for mercy to implore
For the home I loved of yore.
Hearts are grieving
Past retrieving
Land farewell for evermore.

Anonymous,
Tros y Garreg,
translated by H. F. Bantock.

IX RELIGIOUS AND ECONOMIC EXILE FROM WALES

Sometimes the motive for leaving the beloved homeland was the greater urgency for freedom to practice the religion of choice —but at the price of constant *hiraeth* for what was left behind.

44.
　　　Although this place [Milan] is fair, and although it is pleasant to see the green leaves giving shade from the heat of day and delightful to feel this north breeze blowing under the vine branches to gladden our hearts in this excessive warmth so depressing to one born and raised in such a cold country as Wales, yet I have *hiraeth* for many things which were to be had in Wales to pass the time entertainingly and happily when sheltering from the heat on a long summer's day. For there, however warm the weather, all kinds of men could find peace and entertainment. If one wanted to be amused, one could find a minstrel and his harp to play gentle airs, or a singer of sweet ditties to sing with the strings whatever one might wish for, be it to praise virtue or to revile evil. If you wished to hear about the customs of the country in the times of our grandfathers, there would be grey-haired old men who would relate to you by word of mouth every remarkable and worthy deed done in the land of Wales for a long time. But if you wished to study and read by yourself, you could chose a suitable place to do so, however warm the weather, either in summerhouses, or by running waters in a dale of young trees, or in a fertile valley, or on a sloping clover-covered meadow, or in a glade of birch or ash trees, or on an open, breezy mountain, or in some other place where there would be neither weariness nor fatigue caused by the heat of the weather. But in this town there are no such things; for if you enter a cave or a cove where the sun never shines, you will get a deadly chill; if, then, you stay in an open place, you will find that the heat there melts even the crows and the birds; if you stay in the house, the sultriness will choke you; and as for these vineyards, although they look delightful, and

although it is more pleasant to tarry here than anywhere else about us, yet a Welshman's heart does not warm to them as it would to the banks of the Dee, or to the Clwyd Valley, or to a number of places which I could name from St. David's to Holyhead in Anglesey. And even if this place were comparable to the most pleasant district in Wales, yet there would be more joy in my heart if I heard the cuckoo singing in Wales than there would be here if I heard the sweet songs of the nightingale or the gentle voice of the thrush or the bright tunes of the blackbird, or indeed should all the birds of the world join together to sing a constant chorus of paradisean music.

Dr. Gruffudd Robert,
(exiled to Milan by his religion in the 16th century),
Welsh Grammar : Prologue,
translated by Gwynn ap Gwilym.

More often, Welshmen were driven from home by economic hardships exacerbated by English domination of Wales. Sometimes they were forced into the industrialised and anglicised South; sometimes into the plains and towns of England. But material improvement seldom made up for the *hiraeth* of separation.

45.

There are in London clever men, there is in London every joy, there is in London cure for all ills except *hiraeth.*

Traditional folk verse,
translated by Gwynn ap Gwilym.

46.

After the train had started, Dafydd closed his eyes. The separation had been long and tedious, and he was glad it was over . . . His thoughts revolved in a circle and returned to the same place—small wages or no work at all, leaning on his family and worrying, or leaving in search of work, existing or living, living or existing. At last the scales had fallen in favour of leaving. He tried to remember the host of young men who had left home since the beginning of the century: some, like himself, for the South, some for America;

some returning because they had failed to settle down from *hiraeth*; others coming back on a visit with gold in their teeth and top-coats down to their feet, their Welsh affected, everything suggesting that they were doing well for themselves. That too, perhaps, was an attempt to hide *hiraeth*. He preferred the first lot, those who had broken their hearts and come back soon.

He could not forget Alis's face last night as they bade farewell; her eyes were alight with hope and fearless yearning to join him in the South and to settle there. As he thought of this, his heart became a lump of ice; he was not going to the South to settle down; he was going there with the hope of coming back. Alis, however, was an orphan, serving at a hard farm for five pounds per half year. She would not have to pluck hard at the roots if she left; to start again somewhere new would be heaven for her. That morning in his bed in the loft, his nose almost touching the roof, he had almost changed his mind and stayed at home when he considered that he might never again descend the ladder to the warm kitchen, wash in the back yard, and breakfast on the bright, comfortable hearth.

As the train ran along the coast, dawn was approaching; the clouds hung like shreds of sacking, zigzag above the cold, grey sea, and the sea itself glittered up to the foam on the edge of the sand. He felt hungry. He had in his pocket a packet of sandwiches which his mother had cut. She had put a white cloth around them, like an envelope, and secured the cloth with a safety-pin from her shawl. He was afraid to open it. In the packet was his home and everything it represented. In it too was the thread which bound him to these things and which plucked him back to them, the thread which had held him for so many years and which gave him so much pain when he pulled the other way to free himself. He knew, if only he opened the packet, that this thing—this bond— would be there in the bread-and-butter. The roots had burrowed down deeply and *hiraeth* was sprouting on the twigs. When a fellow-traveller offered him a sandwich, he had to refuse and open his own packet. The pressure-marks of his mother's fingers were on the bread, and he nearly choked.

Kate Roberts,
The Journey,
translated by Gwynn ap Gwilym.

Tomb of Llywelyn Fawr, Gwydir Chapel, Llanrwst, Gwynedd.

Holyhead Harbour, Anglesey, Gwynedd.

Yes, William Tan y Chwarel's letter had shaken John Roberts's mind considerably today. William would write to John once in a while to tell him how things were going in the Quarry and in the old district. His letter always cheered his old pal, but the one he had received yesterday had had a different effect. Not that John was sad, but it was easy for his wife to see that he was ready to pack up and return to the North. She had known these signs ever since she had first come to the South . . .

And now, as he sat by the fireside, before starting off for the night-shift, he was as restless and as ready to nag as a bee in a fox-glove . . .

"I sometimes long to return to the North, Elin," said John.

"Do you ?" (without lifting her head).

"Yes indeed, girl. I'm like a fish out of water in the colliery."

Kate Roberts,
Hiraeth,
translated by Gwynn ap Gwilym.

X THE HIRAETH OF EMIGRANTS TO AMERICA

Over the past few centuries impoverished Welshmen emigrated to America in droves. A forward-looking *hiraeth* for the freedom and security that the new land represented competed with the desolate *hiraeth* of life-long banishment from the cherished land.

48.

It was a sad journey my coming to this country (Virginia). A hundred times I have talked about and pined for the foam-washed shores of lovely Gwynedd.

> Goronwy Owen (1723-1769),
> *Elegy on Lewis Morris.*

49.

Consider . . . Goronwy's *hiraeth* for Anglesey :

Great is my grief for her,
Anglesey is like Zion to me;
My life will not be comforted
Without Anglesey, despite every song or chord.

It matters not how much singing or how much dancing there may be, says Goronwy, my soul's lament for Anglesey will not be silenced. Why for Anglesey ? Anglesey is quite a commonplace and unromantic land, its bones protruding through its flesh in many a place. It has no expansive, fertile valleys, or romantic dales, or wide rivers, or high mountains. Why should the poet bruise his soul with *hiraeth* for Anglesey? Ah! it was in Anglesey that he was born and raised, it was there that his mother taught him to talk, it was there that the paths were which he had walked as a child. And he had to leave Anglesey for Liverpool and London and America without ever seeing his dear old country again, and *hiraeth* for it remained a terrible bitterness in his soul.

> John Owen, Morfa Nefyn,
> *Hiraeth am Dduw*,
> sermon translated by Gwynn ap Gwilym.

Of all the inhabitants of earth, it is probably the Celt who is the most inclined to welcome melancholy. At least, that is his reputation beyond Offa's Dyke. He is the most homesick emigrant under the sun, and he is not always sure why. He is such a vague creature. "He journeyed not knowing where he would set up camp," said Machreth of him when describing his early pilgrimages. He is such a passionate creature, too— passionate in exultation, passionate in despair.

Dewi Emrys (1881-1952),
Y Falen,
translated by Gwynn ap Gwilym.

51.

Letter from Charles Evans, late of Merthyr, at New Pittsburgh Mines, St. Louis. March 11, 1898.

We left the Land of our Fathers on 10 February and about forty of the children of Wales arrived safely in Liverpool that night from different parts of Glamorgan with each one of us feeling bruised in our hearts.

Letter from John Lloyd at 63 Chrysler Street, New York, to his parents in Pontralltgoch near Llanelwy. August 1, 1868.

Talking about going to America and actually going are two different things. Many of my friends came to see me off down the river. They looked worriedly at me and I at them. It was a shaky first step from the landing stage onto the ship. As we sailed those who were left behind waved their handkerchiefs, their hands and their hats above their heads. Oh! oh! there was Liverpool disappearing from our sight. Soon we could see the shores of Flintshire, and when opposite Rhyl, ah! there was the dear Clwyd Valley as if opening before me and a feeling of *hiraeth* came over me when I remembered that Pont'rallt goch lay in that direction and as I caught sight of the haunts of my youth I shed a tear.

Goodnight O land of my birth,
You are fading in the twilight,
The wind complains and on the shore,
The waves roar to utter destruction,
The sun sets beyond the waters,
I will follow it before the wind,
And for a time I will leave you my dear country.

Alan Conway,
The Welsh in America.

52.

(The three friends are walking up to the summit of the Allegheny Mountains, and they have journeyed nearly four hundred miles.)

". . . If there was a lake here, I'd drink it all, every drop of it. What a terrible thirst! If all the cows of Llanbryn Mair were milked at the same time, I'd drink their milk before it was out of their teats . . . And I could swallow all the flummery that's in the cauldrons of Llanbryn Mair . . . Think of getting this thirst and hunger in Llanbryn Mair. What a paradise! . . ."

"Poor Siôn, it doesn't do you any good thinking of such a thing. You won't get the milk or the flummery. So there!"

"Worse luck, Seciel, worse luck. No milk, no flummery . . . no buttermilk or porridge; no oatcake or wheat bread, and no bacon. Nothing! No, none of the fruits of the old country. Only its *hiraeth*—hunger and thirst for it. As in the old stanza :

Hiraeth, hiraeth, leave me, leave me,
Do not press so hard upon me;
To the wall I turn my face, so
If my heart breaks, let it be so."

"Good heavens, Siôn, let's sing it. And you too, Seciel. The three of us. What about it? The first Welsh singing ever heard on this mountain!"

"You're wrong there, my lad. I sang here once before when I came here to look the place over for Morgan John

Rhys. This is the exact spot where he intends to establish his 'Welsh Colony' if he's successful . . . It's on these hills that he's going to build his home . . . There then!"

"Goodness gracious . . . you don't say so! Well, I'll never budge."

"Won't you, Ned? Well, I will, as soon as I can!"

"Why, Siôn? It's not so unlike Wales as you see it from the top of Newydd Fynyddog."

"No. That's just it. After coming so far, damn it, I want to see a completely different country. Every hill and tree I see here is so very similar to those at home, they turn this *hiraeth* within me into wild pangs."

Ambrose Bebb (1894-1955),
Dial y Tir,
translated by Gwynn ap Gwilym.

53. (Joseph Parry is leaving Wales for America).

I should have mentioned the singing of a number of Betty's favourite hymns by those who came in crowds to see her off but that goes without saying anyway. Where the train goes round the bend just outside the town Betty leaned out of the window-space of the compartment and took one look backwards towards the town of Tydfil the Martyr. Then she sat down and composed herself. Her four children had a corner seat apiece and before long the novelty of the first train-ride of their lives made them forget some of the pain of the week's leave-taking. Only Joseph was without eyes to see the places they travelled through on the way to Cardiff. His eyes were too full of the town that was in his heart, the town of Tydfil the Martyr. He sniffed when he set foot in Cardiff, from where they were to sail on the good ship *Jane Anderson*. This is not half the town Merthyr is, he said, and he was right. Some Welsh people of the same denomination, the Welsh 'independents', whose home and whose chapel was in Cardiff, were putting them up for the night.

Next morning they went aboard the ship, the sailing-ship, the *Jane Anderson*. Same name as our Jane, mam, said Henry. Yes, said Betty quietly before closing her eyes to pray briefly where she stood, with bag and baggage and children around her. Whilst she prayed silently Joseph looked up at the seagulls that were sweeping, diving and climbing above and about the ship's sails. They never flew inland as far as the town of Tydfil the Martyr, now twenty-five miles away, Joseph thought with regret. Already he was longing for his home-town, longing for it with that intense kind of longing which we Welsh call ' hiraeth '. The sight and smell of the sea, the seagulls crowding the air above the ship, other little ships like the one he was on taking on passengers, coal, iron and merchandise. Sailors hoisting and lowering sails and coiling ropes whilst others went on loading and unloading the ships.

Jack Jones (1884-1970),
Off to Philadelphia in the Morning.

54.

It is Merthyr is on the boy's stomach all the time, Betty explained. Naturally, said Daniel. But he will learn. Hiraeth will give way to pride before long. By ' hiraeth ' Daniel meant that intense longing for Wales which, as we have said before perhaps, afflicts us Welshmen when there is water between us and Wales.

Jack Jones,
Off to Philadelphia in the Morning.

55.

At the end of the century there were in the United States a hundred thousand natives of Wales. Since then the figure has decreased, but it is estimated that if, in addition to those born in Wales, those who have at least one Welsh parent are counted, then the Welsh-Americans of the present-day number a quarter of a million.

Their loss is one which Wales could ill afford and who can estimate the suffering through *hiraeth* for their native land of these Celts in exile? As we have seen, they clung to their language and customs, and they persevered in holding their religious services in Welsh whenever they could. Even today there are Welsh churches in many of the great cities.

David Williams (1900-1978),
Wales and America.

56. LAMENT FOR A LEG (Excerpt)

Near the yew tree under which the body of Dafydd ap Gwilym is buried in Strata Florida, Cardiganshire, there stands a stone with the following inscription: ' The left leg and part of the thigh of Henry Hughes, Cooper, was cut off and interr'd here, June 18, 1756. ' Later the rest of Henry Hughes set off across the Atlantic in search of better fortune.

. . . Soon with my only, my best, foot forward
    I fled, quiet, to far America:

Where, with my two tried hands, I plied
My trade and, true, in time made good
Though grieving for Pontrhydfendigaid.
Sometimes, all at once, in my tall cups,
I'd cry in *hiraeth* for my remembered thigh
Left by the grand yew in Ystrad Fflur's
Bare ground, near the good bard . . .

John Ormond.

XI WELSH EMIGRANTS TO PATAGONIA AND THE DOMINIONS

Other parts of the world also offered economic hope to the needy Welsh, but always at great cost in *hiraeth :*

57. They not only desired to escape from the oppression and the poverty, but also to create a new nation across the sea. The name they gave to this dreamland was Y Wladfa . . . Many parties of Welshmen were sent out from time to time with the intention of establishing this colony in the United States. Strong Welsh societies flourished there; chapels were built, eisteddfodau held, and books and newspapers published, all in the Welsh language. Unfortunately, the children of these settlers tended to become more American than Welsh. On this account there arose a desire among the Welshmen in America to go to . . . Patagonia.

Within twenty years of the first group's arrival, the settlement had become a great success, and the dream of a Free Wales was being realised. Chapels had been built, and religion continued to flourish. The culmination of literary activity was the annual chair eisteddfod, with its own Gorsedd of Bards, its chaired bard and choirs exactly as in Wales . . .

A gradual but constant change has come to the life of the settlement during the last half century. Emigration from Wales ceased in 1912, and people of different nations have flocked there. By today the population of the province is about 150,000 but only about 20,000 of these are descendants of the Welsh, of whom about 5,000 speak Welsh and keep alive the old traditions of their fathers. Most of these live together, either in the Vale of Camwy or in Cwm Hyfryd . . . Some of these young people visited Wales recently, and although they are of the fourth generation, and not one of their family had visited Wales for a century, their Welsh is better than that of those of us who live here.

R. Bryn Williams,
The Welsh Colony in Patagonia.
(pp. 15, 43, 71, 73)

58.

"Welcome to the Colony of Camwy," she said, in the Old Language. "May your visit be happy for every moment and all trouble only a dream . . . It is lovely to talk to somebody from home. I am going, now just. But I will never believe it. I am in shivers to be there before the snowdrops have gone. And to see the primroses and crocus. I will put my face to them for hours."

But sorrow was in me, because I knew that her dream was late, and the snowdrops were long past, and the primrose and crocus would be gone. She wondered if it would be a great change to go back to the Old Land that she had left thirty-five years before with her mother and father among the other pioneers, and she pointed up the Bay of Nymphs to the narrow beach and the cliffs where the sailing ship *Mimosa* had landed them. That year was before I was born, but white hair and wrinkled or not, I felt that she was much younger than I had ever been.

Richard Llewellyn,
Up, Into The Singing Mountain.

59.

Old William Barnett, who died last year out on the Saskatchewan prairie, where he went as a pioneer in 1910, remembered vividly his childhood journey on the gambo to the Fair from his father's farm above Beguildy in the eighteen-eighties accompanied by a Granny steeped in local folklore and stories which at times flashed back over the centuries to tell of prisoners who were tried at Bryndraenog and sent to Ludlow ' to be hung by a Bishop '—stories, indeed, which linked Bryndraenog's fine fifteenth-century cruck-built hall with the harsh justice that Roland Lee meted out as President of the Council of Wales and the Marches in Henry VIII's reign.

Old folk's memories have declined, as the May Fairs have declined. A century of rural depopulation has worn them thin . . .

In some ways the most vivid recollections have been recorded by those, like William Barnett, who have moved away to sharply contrasting scenes and societies, and have preserved the old community unaltered in their memories. The memories of most Welsh emigrants might be suspect as

sources tinged with *hiraeth* for a ' never-never-land ' far away,
but Barnett's childhood and schooldays were recalled with a
bitter tinge that sharpened their clarity.   There was no
question of an imposed elementary education in a foreign
tongue, for England had become dominant in Radnorshire
long before the second half of the nineteenth century . . .

Frank Noble,
Radnorshire.

60. ASKING

Does watercress still grow as thick now near St. Donat's
  Castle?
And do the falls still catch the light up in Ffestiniog vale?
Is it morning in the singing of the choir at Treorchy?
Do the sermons at Machynlleth go on thrilling through
  their *hwyl*?

Is Richard Hughes still writing within cuckoo call of Snow-
  don?
Are the bells of Penmark church heard off at Rhoose now
  through the rain?
Shall Welsh go on like Brecon women joking at the shuttle ?
Wales . . . O is it Wales now in this wanderer's heart again?

Godfrey John,
(Welsh-born Canadian citizen),
Five Seasons.

61. Memoir of Beatrice Spooner-Jones Levertoff, mother of
Denise Levertov.

After she left Wales in 1910 to go to Constantinople she
never really lived there again, though of course she visited
from time to time, the last occasion being just after my
father's death in 1955. But she has never lost a great love for
and pride in Wales. The Welsh hymns, and secular songs
like *Daffyth y Garreg Wen*, sung or remembered or heard on
records, never fail to bring tears to her eyes. One of her great
joys in Oaxaca (Mexico) in the days when she was still
strong and agile enough (i.e. into her 80s) was to go ' for a
good tramp ' on the grassy hills just above the town, remin-
iscent of Welsh moorland . . .

Denise Levertov, *An American Poet with a Russian
Name Tells About the Life of her* 100% *Welsh Mother.*

XII THE WANDERING WELSH
AND AMBIVALENT HIRAETH

Not all emigration has been the result of constraint, whether political, economic or religious. Moving along is as Welsh a trait as staying put. The original Celtic migrations stopped only when the western seaboard was reached, and not even then, if recent claims about early Celtic monuments in America are ever proved.

Certainly a strong sea-faring tradition lies behind such legends as the Welsh St. Malo's voyage with St. Brendan to seek the Isle of the Blessed or the Fortunate Islands in the West, and Prince Madoc's sailing to the Western Hemisphere. There may be in the Welsh temperament a perpetual tension between staying and leaving, a yearning for something better, a grief for something left behind.

62.   This is a good country . . . At present there is plenty of land and whoever comes has plenty of choice . . . For those afflicted with homesickness the best advice is to stay at home.

Letter from John Newell Lewis, late of Capel Dewi Uchaf, Carmarthen, in Capel Aska, Shell Creek, Columbus, Platte County, Nebraska, to his countrymen. February 12, 1873, Alan Conway, *The Welsh in America.*

63.   Welshmen . . . in whose fiery love for their own land no hatred for another finds a place.

Proverb.

64.   Fits of longing for wandering come over the Welsh period-ically as they came over the Danes—caused by scarcity of food and density of population, or by a sense of oppression and yearning for freedom. An empty stomach sometimes, and sometimes a fiery imagination, sent a crowd of advent-urers to new lands . . .

O. M. Edwards (1858-1920),
A Short History of Wales.

65.

Despite their love of their native land, of its farms and villages, of its churches and chapels, the Welsh people have never been unwilling to leave home. They have followed the sea and become familiar with strange lands and peoples. This has made it easier for them to settle down in new countries. Many, it is true, have been driven from their homes by the poverty of the hilly soil to seek a better livelihood in places where nature has been kinder. But many have left from no motive other than to seek adventure and to see the wonders of the world.

David Williams (1900-1978),
Wales and America.

66.

(William Morris Hughes, born of Welsh parents, and educated in Llandudno Grammar School, then London, decided, because of deafness, against a teaching career in favour of emigration to Australia where he became Prime Minister at a time when another Welshman, Lloyd George, was British Prime Minister).

The Celtic temperament . . . began to make itself felt about this period—the "long, long dream of youth," the restlessness, the beckoning shadows of dim, far-off, half-forgotten things. As he himself summed it up on one occasion: "The sight of the colliers at Lambeth fired my imagination. I liked to go down to London Bridge to see the ships that went out to sea. Accompanied by another boy named Payne, I would frequently go down to the East India Docks to see the ships that went to Australia. At last we made up our mind that we, too, would go forth in one."

They landed in Brisbane in 1884. Hughes was then a lad of twenty—with no friends, save the boy Payne. He had no money, no influence, only a stock of bad health happily backed by a lively belief in himself that no trials or calamities have ever been able to throw into complete eclipse. And, although he knew it not, he had, in the mere act of emigration, made his first great step upward to a sphere of dazzling brilliance and usefulness.

Stanhope W. Sprigg,
W. M. Hughes, The Strong Man of Australia.

XIII FORKED OR BLACK HIRAETH OF THE SELF-EXILE

In more recent times the prime motivation for emigration has been ambition for material success. This quest for opportunity for personal expansion has often created in the wandering Welshman a deep conflict in his loyalties, leading to an ambiguous, bitter form of *hiraeth* that might be termed "forked" or "black" *hiraeth*, since it is based on a love hate relationship to country and kin, and a miserable state of self-division that is emotionally ravaging, giving the lie to the old proverb:

Amser a dangnofa bob hiraeth—Time soothes all longing

67.

> It was funny. The more he went about America the more he longed for Wales, and after seven years in Wales he longed to go to America to open his lungs and get his mind swept clear of all the sand his people had thrown into the machinery of his prolific mind. He wanted to get away from the pressure of his own people, from their jealous pride in him, from all the petty restrictions which Welsh Nonconformity imposed upon him. Yet before he had been a month in America he was longing for Wales, so what could you do with man like that?

> Jack Jones (1884-1970),
> *Off to Philadelphia in the Morning.*

68. STORMY NIGHT IN NEWCASTLE, N.S.W.

Rain thrashes the house, and I am back
Where such a ruffian night would lullaby
Me to a dreamless sleep. I lie
And listen to the wind's threat and crack,

And cry, I am not homesick, am not sick
For hills so sodden with such rain
And wind their absence is a pain,
A calm day makes us wish a storm come quick.

No, it is too easy to remember, now
When just a harmless lash of rain
Can keep me from my sleep, that then
I could have slept as sound as other men
Through better storms than this, nor wondered how
A sleeper in such storms would wake again.

T. Harri Jones (1921-1965).

69.   LAND OF MY FATHERS

Some frosty farmers fathered me to fare
Where their dreams never led, the sunned and blue
Salt acres where Menelaus once made ado
Because Paris also thought Helen was fair;
And now this ancient sunburnt country where
Everything's impossibly bright and new
Except what happens between me and you
When I ransack your bright and ravished hair.

Always I feel the cold and cutting blast
Of winds that blow about my native hills,
And know that I can never be content
In this or any other continent
Until with my frosty fathers I am at last
Back in the old country that sings and kills.

T. Harri Jones

XIV HIRAETH FOR PERSONS— FOR LOVED ONES LEFT OR LOST

Some of the most powerful poetry of *hiraeth* is *hiraeth* for persons. Those left behind may suffer *hiraeth* as much as those who have gone away. Stayers and leavers share this type of *hiraeth* equally. First, a group of poems by the lovelorn :

70.

I have *hiraeth* for my country, I have *hiraeth* for my father,
I have even more *hiraeth* for the girl whom I love.

Traditional harp stanza, translated by
Gwynn ap Gwilym.

Mae arnaf hiraeth am fy ngwlad,
Mae arnaf hiraeth am fy nhad;
Mae arnaf hiraeth mwy na hynny
Am y ferch yr wy' 'n ei charu.

71.

I have a great *hiraeth* for someone
Though I have not mentioned it to anyone;
And so does he, so beautiful his moods,
Have a great *hiraeth* for me.

Traditional harp stanza.

Mae arnaf hiraeth mawr am rywun,
Er na sonias air wrth undyn.
Mae arno yntau, hardd ei foddau,
Hiraeth mawr amdanaf innau.

72.

The one who has my heart
Lives far away from here
And *hiraeth* to see her
Is making me wan.

Tra Bo Dau, traditional song.

Mae'r hon a gâr fy nghalon i
Ymhell oddi yma'n byw,
A hiraeth am ei gweled hi
A gwna yn ddrwg fy lliw.

73.

My memory lingers in her company,
longing for her whilst she hates me.
Though I may do the girl honour by my praise,
suffering doesn't help me.

Hywel ab Owain Gwynedd (12th century),
Awdl III,
translated by Gwyn Williams.

74.

. . .Great stress that concerns me besets me
And longing, alas, that goes with it
For Nest, fair as an apple-blossom,
For Perweur, centre of my sin,
For pure Generys, who cured not my lust,
    May she not remain chaste,
    For Hunydd, concern till doomsday,
    For Hawis, my choice for courtship.

Hywel ab Owain Gwynedd,
Gorhoffedd Hywel ab Owain,
Section *In Praise of Fair Women*,
translated by Joseph P. Clancy.

64

75.

Blessed would I be if I could see
Seven children, five not yet walking,
Four cradles on the floor at one time,
By the man who caused this *hiraeth*.

Traditional harp stanza.

Gwyn fy myd na chawn i weled
Saith o blant, a phump heb gerdded,
Pedwar crud ar lawr ar unwaith
Gan y mab a'm rhoes mewn hiraeth.

76. LONGING

Longing! leave my heart for an hour
    and turn away awhile
to tell my yellow-topped girl
    that here's a man for whom the world is vile.

Anonymous 16th century englyn,
translated by Gwyn Williams.

HIRAETH

Dos ymaith hiraeth orig o'm calon,
    cilia i ffwrdd ychydig;
dywed i'm gwen felenfrig
fod dyn ac arno fyd dig.

77. OH ! COME BACK HOME

Painful my heart, oh, faded my beauty,
Where are you, my dear, tarrying so long;
The children are waiting for you every minute of the day,
And I, too, am anxious and my mind sad.

Oh, come back home, Oh, come back home,
If I knew where you were, I would fly to fetch you.

You used to be always meek and merry,
The *hiraeth* around me is consuming my breast;
Oh, come home to your cottage shelter by the stream,
To cheer the hearts of your wife and your children.

Oh, come back home, Oh, come back home,
If I knew where you were, I would fly to fetch you.

Talhaiarn (John Jones, 1810-1869).

O, TYRED YN OL

Dolurus fy nghalon, o gwelw fy mhryd,
P'le 'rwyt ti f'anwylyd yn aros cyhŷd;
Mae'r plant yn dy ddisgwyl bob munud o'r dydd,
A minau'n bryderus a'm meddwl yn brudd.

O! tyred yn ôl, O! tyred yn ôl,
Pe gwyddwn lle'r ydwyd ehedwn i'th nôl.

Yr oeddit bob amser yn llariaidd a llon,
Mae hiraeth am danad yn ysu fy mron ;
O ! tyr'd i dy fwthyn yng nghysgod y nant,
I lonni calonnau dy wraig a dy blant.

O! tyred yn ôl, O! tyred yn ôl,
Pe gwyddwn lle'r ydwyd ehedwn i'th nôl.

XV HIRAETH FOR THE DEAD

Separation by death has produced some of the most heart-rending poetry of *hiraeth*. The elegiac tradition is very strong in Welsh literature.

78.

Hiraeth came like an arrow to my heart
With a crop of deep sighs
When I realised that my beloved
Was in the dust in the parish of Llanllechid.

Traditional harp stanza,
translated by Gwen Watts Jones.

Hiraeth ddaeth fel saeth i'm calon
Gyda chnwd o ddwys och'neidion,
Pan ganfyddwn fod f'anwylyd
Yn y llwch ym mhlwyf Llanllechid.

79.

She died of *hiraeth*
Of *hiraeth* for Hywel
Myfanwy died in Castle Dinas Brân . . .

Cariad y Bardd,
traditional song.

Bu farw o hiraeth
O hiraeth am Hywel,
Bu farw Myfanwy yng Nghaer Dinas Brân . . .

I have *hiraeth* tonight for the hands that drummed on the chimney-corner after a day's work, strong restless hands, bearing the powerful currents of the soil.

I long to see again those hands snatching cap and crook to foretell "a little stroll", the hand that shaded the eyes from daylight as he gazed at the sheep across the glen, an old shepherd imprisoned by lameness.

I have *hiraeth* for that hand on my shoulder: "You see my dark girl . . ." when the song was over, and for their confident movement as he discussed some hymn-tune. If the voice was husky and the breath failing, their beat on the arm of the big chair was constant. My hands were flesh from the flesh of their assurance,—hands that had ploughed, that had toiled.

I have *hiraeth* for the hands that sometimes wandered to reach for a frail, old photograph from a pocket, a photograph of a long-haired girl in the corn harvest when the days were long and golden-yellow; he reaped enjoyment from her company.

I even have *hiraeth* for the hands that were like feathers on a strange coverlet with no more sighing in them any more.

Let those hands be crossed tonight. The soil here is easy and light upon them. Their day is withered.

Nesta Wyn Jones, *Taid*,
translated by Gwynn ap Gwilym.

Mae gen i hiraeth, heno,
Am y dwylo
Fyddai'n drymio ar y pentan
Adeg noswyl.
Y dwylo cryf, aflonydd,
Cryf eu ffrwd, o gofio'r pridd.

Mae gen i hiraeth am gael gweld
Y dwylo'n bachu cap â bagl ffon
I ragfynegi "tro bach",
Ac am y llaw gysgodai drem
Yn haul y dydd
Pan syllai ar y da ar draws y cwm.
Hen fugail, cloffni'n garchar.

Mae gen i hiraeth am y llaw
Ar f'ysgwydd : "Weli di, 'rhen hogan ddu . . ."
Wrth orffen cân,
Ac am bendantrwydd eu symudiad hwy
Wrth drafod tôn rhyw emyn.
Os bloesg y llais, os pallai anadl,
Cyson eu curiad hwy ar fraich y gadair fawr,
A'm dwylo i oedd gnawd o gnawd
Eu sicrwydd hwy,
Dwylo fu'n troi, fu'n trin.

Mae gen i hiraeth am y dwylo
Grwydrai, ambell waith,
I estyn llun bach bregus, hen o boced,
Llun geneth hirwallt yn y c'naeaf ŷd
Pan oedd y dyddiau'n faith
Ac eto'n felyn aur bob un,
Medi mwynhad o'i chwmni.

Mae gen i hiraeth, hyd yn oed,
Am ddwylo fu fel plu
Ar gwrlid dieithr,
Heb ochenaid ynddynt, mwy . . .

Plether y dwylo, heno,
Hawdd yw'r pridd
Ac ysgafn yma drostynt.
Gwyw eu dydd.

81.

Siôn's death stands near me
like two barbs in my breast.
My son, child of my hearth,
my breast, my heart, my song,
my one delight before my death,
my knowing poet, my luxury;
my jewel, and my candle,
my sweet soul, my one betrayal,
my chick learning my song,
my chaplet of Iseult, my kiss,
my nest, (woe that he's gone!)
my lark, my little wizard.

69

My Siôn, my bow, my arrow,
my suppliant, my boyhood,
Siôn who sends to his father
a sharpness of longing and love.

Lewis Glyn Cothi (15th century),
Elegy on his son Siôn,
translated by Gwyn Williams.

Yngo y saif angau Siôn
yn ddeufrath yn y ddwyfron.
Fy mab, fy muarth baban,
fy mron, fy nghalon, fy nghân
fy mryd cyn fy marw ydoedd,
fy mardd doeth, fy moeth im oedd;
fy nhegan oedd, fy nghannwyll,
fy enaid teg, fy un twyll;
fy nghyw yn dysgu fy nghân,
fy nghae Esyllt, fy nghusan;
fy nyth, gwae fi yn ei ôl,
fy ehedydd, fy hudol;
fy Siôn, fy mwa, fy saeth,
f'ymbiliwr, fy mabolaeth;
Siôn y sy'n danfon i'w dad
awch o hiraeth a chariad.

82.

I know a lad slain by grief's pain—Mary,
  Pentraeth's gold candle's dead!—
Made weak by a, woe's poison,
Gossamer face, nursed on mead.

. . .

Garbed, wine-lavish sun, near Cyrchell's white strand,
  In a new grave's close cell;
Grieved he, since heaven is hers,
Who loved her with fierce longing.

Gruffudd ap Maredudd (14th century),
Lament for Gwenhwyfar,
translated by Joseph P. Clancy.

Gwn feinwas a las o loes hiraeth,—Fair,
    Farw eurgannwyll Bentraeth,
    Gwan yn ôl, gwenwyn alaeth,
    Gwawn wedd, gwin a medd a'i maeth.

. . .

Gwisgwyd haul gwindraul ger gwyndraeth—Cyrchell
    Mewn carchar glasfedd caeth;
    Gwae ef, i gain nef gan aeth,
    A'i carawdd rhag dig hiraeth.

With his keen feeling for nature, the Welshman has a way of reading in natural objects the "signatures" of his longing, or projecting his *hiraeth* onto animals and birds.

83.

Singer of deathless song, longing in its voice,
　　Soaring with the motion of the hawk;
　　Eloquent cuckoo in Aber Cuawg.

The Poetry of Llywarch Hen (6th century),
translated by Patrick K. Ford.

Cethlydd cathl fodawg, hiraethawg ei llef,
　　Taith oddef tuth hebawg;
　　Cog freuer yn Aber Cuawg.

84.

My love is like a cloudy thunderclap on the horizons of my longing.

I do not hear the rustle of the wind in the corn, the lamb in the orchard, the scream in the night; I cannot digest the summer moon and its crumbs the stars without remembering my love, how she used to be sad on the scattered horizons of my longing.

T. Glynne Davies,
Adfeilion,
translated by R. Gerallt Jones.

Y mae fy nghariad
Fel taran gymylog ar orwelion fy hiraeth.

Ni chlywaf siffrwd y gwynt yn yr ŷd,
Yr oen yn y berllan,
Y sgrech yn y nos;

Ni fedraf dreulio lleuad yr haf
A'i briwsion,
Y sêr,
Heb gofio fu nghariad,
Fel y byddai'n drist
Ar orwelion ulw fy hiraeth.

85. FOLKSONGS OF WANDERERS

I   Titrwm, tatrwm, Gwen, the hue of the lambs,
Hue of the fair Trefoil, I am knocking.
Cold is the blast across the lake,
O flower of the vale, awake!
Blow the fire it will kindle soon,
The weather is tempestuous tonight.

Sometimes in London, sometimes in Chester,
I labour hard to gain her;
Sometimes I hold her in my arms.
Sometimes I'm far, far from her.
I would caress the lovely rose
If I were now to meet her.

If far away from Wales I go,
What shall I do with my girl?
Take her with me o'er the sea
Or leave her, a-longing?

My heart flies back from every land
To the hills and vales of Pentraeth.

II   Swallow, swallow, flitting so joyously
from the eaves of my house
when thou returnest over the waves of the ocean
carry my love to my dear maid;
Longing, longing (Hiraeth, hiraeth) fills my heart
to see my darling Gwen, colour of the rose;
Remember me to the beauteous maid.

III   Thou Sun that seest on thy journey
Every corner of the world,
Tell me, if thou hast the language
How fares my sheltered Wales?

86.

I listened to the nightingale and longed for the shy one,
the spear was deep-hued, my mind wandered far;
the girl is not asleep, I know how far.

Gwalchmai (12th century),
Gorhoffedd (Exultation),
translated by Gwyn Williams.

Endeweisy eaws am ryhiraeth yr gwyl,
gweilgig porfor, pwyllad uyuyr;
pell nad hunawc gwenn, gogwn pa hyr.

87.

In the sea there is a fish,
And on the shore I seek it.
In the school there is learning,
And in my little heart there is longing.

Traditional folksong, translated by the
Welsh Folk Song Society.

Yn y mor y mae pysgodyn,
Ac ar y traeth yr wy'n ei 'mofyn.
Yn yr ysgol mae dysgeidiaeth,
Ac ar fy nghalon fach mae hiraeth.

88.

As I walk out at break of day,
My poor heart becomes sad
As I hear the little birds sing,
A longing comes for fair Eliza.

When in the evening I take a walk,
My poor heart melts like wax,
As I hear the little birds sing,
A great longing comes for fair Eliza.

When in the garden I walk forth,
Amongst the flowers that are so beautiful,
And when I cut the little primroses
A great longing comes for fair Eliza.

When in the midst of gladness
I feel a pain in my bosom;
When I hear the sound of the slender harpstrings,
A great longing comes for Eliza.

Traditional folksong, translated by the
Welsh Folk Song Society.

Pan byddwy'n rhodio gyda'r dydd,
Fy nghalon bach sy'n myn'd yn brudd;
Wrth glywed swn yr adar mân,
Daw hiraeth mawr am Lisa lân.

Pan fyddwy'n rhodio gyda'r hwyr
Fy nghalon bach a dôdd fel cwyr;
Wrth glywed swn yr adar mân
Daw hiraeth mawr am Lisa lân.

Pan fyddwy'n rhodio yn yr ardd
Ym mysg y blodau sydd yn hardd,
Yn torri'r mwyn friallu mân
Daw hiraeth mawr am Lisa lân.

Pan fyddwy mewn llawenydd llon,
Fe fydd poenau dan fy mron;
Wrth glywed swn y tannau mân,
Daw hiraeth mawr am Lisa lân.

89.

The eighty years of her eyes stared at the nostalgic sun of
Pen Nant as it set, drawing the sky after it to the heather bed
of the unimpassioned mountain.

T. Glynne Davies,
Adfeilion,
translated by R. Gerallt Jones

75

Syllai pedwar ugain mlynedd ei llygaid
Ar haul hiraethus
Pen Nant yn machlud
Gan hudo'r awyr ar ei ôl
I wely grug
Y mynydd annirwyn.

90.   A MESSAGE HOME

Fly to Wales, my little songbird,
Take a message will you please
From this place of wrath and carnage
To the land of song and peace.
Though here Struma's running sweetly
In the moonlight as of yore,
You'd forget it all completely
If you'd seen the Menai shore.

And how will you be knowing
The place that you must greet?
Fly till you see the mountains
With the waters at their feet,
Where the summer lingers longest,
Where the air is fresh and free,
Where the sea and sky are clearest,
That's Wales, my heart's country.

Fly till you find an island
Where you need no longer roam,
Where the cuckoo's song is earliest,
You'll be welcome, you'll be home.
Fly northward from Brynsiencyn
Do not dawdle by the Tŵr
And make your nest in Traffwll
In the garden of Glan Dŵr.

It's a garden full of blossom,
No fairer garden grows,
And there you'll meet with someone
Who is fairer than a rose.

Sing my sadness, sing to Megan,
Sing as sweetly as you may,
Sing till she feels the hiraeth
That burns my heart away.

And will you tell my cousin
I'd give the world for half an hour
To go fishing in the Traffwll
Far from the sound of war.
Together we'd go rowing
In the quiet starlight then,
Me with Megan and beside him
The girl from Allwadd Wen.

Once you'd sung to Wil and Megan
You'd want to stay, I'm sure.
Who'd come back to Macedonia
From the garden of Glan Dŵr?

Harri Webb,
(from the Welsh of Cynan, 1895-1970).

91. SEEING THE WIND

§ I

It is said that pigs can see the wind,—who knows? My grandmother had seen ghosts and fairies, and had heard singing in the air. I neither saw nor heard any such things, as far as I know. And yet, I have to believe her. Are there not senses that have been lost or become rather dulled? We know not what we can achieve; was not every worthwhile thing that man ever did achieved when man was for a moment more than a man? One must be supernatural for a while before one can accomplish any kind of feat, and one must feel a passion not of this world before one can see the invisible . . .

§ II

Oddly, and yet quite naturally, my starting point from home has always been downhill, and it was downhill that I went sadly enough to start at a new school for the first time, and to spend some weeks away from my family. The delights of expectancy had been long exhausted, and I hated feeling the hill drawing me, as it were, against my will, down to the valley, just as, later on, I hated its holding me back as I climbed up. But I had to get on with it now, and change districts for a time; I had started on my journey and had been escorted part of the way. Superficial smiles of bravery had accompanied the farewells, and I had walked the level mile or more to Pont Cae'r Gors before the real descent began. Near this bridge a new stream starts flowing to the sea, although the sea itself is not in sight. That September day the wind was blowing from the sea to the mountain, and on the top of the hill it came strongly and unashamedly into my face. My eyes became moist. In a flash I realised enviously in what direction it was blowing. I too, almost, saw the wind that day.

§III

One October, a long time ago, I was alone in the midst of strangers on a small steamer sailing at midnight for the Continent from the port of Harwich. For the first time ever I was changing countries for some time, and my loneliness had never been deeper. My eyes were drying with *hiraeth*. The wonder of a new experience had worn thin and had vanished, and the mystery of things to come had not yet engulfed the *hiraeth*. We faced the east and the sea. My feelings were so mixed I did not know exactly what I felt in my heart, but again there blew into my face a hard, piercing wind, and I was most conscious of it. To me, at that time, nothing else existed at all. And there, on that deck, in the passion of realisation, I thought for a moment that I could see the wind.

§IV

It was a dirty July night when we sailed past Holyhead point for a new Continent. Drizzle filled the sky between us and the mountains of Arfon which lay to the left of us, grey and still on their old, unmoving foundations, although they seemed as if they were retreating with a frown. I had half-hoped to see the marvel of sunset over them from the sea for once. But they seemed as if my departure had offended them, and guilt was like a serpent in my breast. I was going far, far away, further than I had ever been, and they had always been so near to me, like some easily-accessible sanctuary. Friendless and down at heart, I stared at them on my left. I was so lonely amongst that mixture of humanity such as one finds aboard ship. Despite the speed of the vessel, I noticed that a strong breeze was blowing across its course towards the dark mountains. And there, between Holyhead and Pen Llŷn, a miracle happened. In the anguish of that night, I am almost certain that I saw the wind.

§V

A time will surely come when I shall depart again—this time leaving home for ever, down hill as I have always gone. And I secretly believe that *hiraeth* will still be smouldering in my heart, and that the sadness of separation will still be pent up within me. But when I reach the end of my journey, and before I am cast into the darkness, it will be very surprising if a gust of wind does not come down through Y Gymwynas* and up Nant Colwyn towards Pont Cae'r Gors. And if it comes—and why shouldn't it?—I am quite certain that the blind, mute, alone and prostrate, at that moment see the wind.

*The Pass of Aberglaslyn

> T. H. Parry-Williams (1887-1975),
> *Ysgrifau*,
> translated by Gwynn ap Gwilym.

92.

The sun knows, the moon knows,
The sea's angry waves know,
The wind knows full well
That the *hiraeth* will never lift from my heart.

> Traditional harp stanza,
> translated by Gwen Watts Jones.

XVII CHIEF BARD OF HIRAETH AND NATURE

Chief bard of *hiraeth* is Dafydd ap Gwilym, who sang of it in love, lamentation and irony.

93. CYWYDD HIRAETH

(An excerpt from a poem in memory of departed colleagues, written for the Dafydd ap Gwilym Society of Oxford University, 1887.)

Dafydd sang divinely of the cuckoo and of the trees, "of sweet birds which loved me and of a girl I saw in the month of May"; of Morfudd and her golden hair, the hair that was more yellow than gold. Without her his song was a song of awkward *hiraeth*; and in winter his poem was one of *hiraeth* for the smile of the summer sun. The heavy note of *hiraeth* was heard so often in his speech: "This will cause me to lie down tonight; *hiraeth*, by Mary, will make me a grave." I too have a grievous *hiraeth* for my gentle friends . . .

Sir John Morris-Jones (1864-1929),
Caniadau,
translated by Gwynn ap Gwilym.

(N.B. *Cywydd* is a Welsh poem in a special metre.)

94.
Her lost life lamenting, I sing broken-hearted,
  Fair as the foam-flake, on grass-blades falling, the bright-
           ness of Builth;
Dear lady unsullied, dispenser of bounty at banquets,
  Of the wine-board's abundance, the patron of poets in their
           pride.
Memories thronging, awakening longing, lie lieger about me,
  My eyes waste for weeping her gem-bright beauty.

Dinas Brân and Plas Newydd, Llangollen, Clwyd.

Nant Gwynant, Gwynedd.

My sorrowful face, tears in torrents bedew it,
Pale and hollow my cheeks, for woe wasting away.
My poison the pain of her loss, my prop and my stay;
She's gone from her palace, no gown of scarlet bedecks me.
Ill work for the eyes is long weeping, the bondage of sorrow,
But worse is the thraldom of longing, the thought of the
loss of Angharad.

Dafydd ap Gwilym (14th century),
Lament for Angharad (his patron's wife),
translated by H. Idris Bell.

Gwedy hoedlddwyn gwŷn wyf geiniad—bronddellt,
Gwedd eiry frisg wisg wellt, gwawr Fuellt fad;
Gwenfun ddiwael, hael heiliad—yng nghyfedd,
Gwinfwrdd a berthedd, gwynfeirdd borthiad.
Gwayw o'i chof trwof trawiad—a'm gwarchae,
Gwae, em oleugae, y mau lygad!
Gwedd, dig argywedd, deigr gawad—a'i gwlych,
Gwyrdd fy ngrudd a chrych, fawrnych farwnad.
Gwenwyn im ei chŵyn, ni chad—i'm ystlys,
Gwanas gywirlys, gŵn ysgarlad.
Gwaith drwg i'r olwg hir wylad—yng nghaeth,
Gwaeth, cyfyng hiraeth, cof Angharad.

95. LOVE'S FEVER

A pretty girl's bewitched me,
Sweet Morfudd, godchild of May.
She'll get her proper greeting,
I'm fevered tonight with love.
She's sown in my breaking heart
Love's seed, a magic frenzy;
The fruits of pain, here's my plaint,
Fair as day, she denies me.
Enchantress, lovely goddess,
Her speech puts a spell on me.
Careless when she is accused,
Careless of me, unfavoured.
Peace I'd have, luck and learning,
Today with my clever girl.

Innocent, unrecompensed,
I'm outlawed from her parish.
It's she who put, most painful,
Longing in her outlaw's heart:
Longer than sea on the strand
Lingers her outlaw's longing.
I've been fettered, my ribs nailed,
Affliction's been my fetter.

Unlikely, my chance of peace
With my shrewd gold-haired maiden:
Bad fevers were bred of this;
Long life for me's unlikely.
She is Ynyr's own offspring;
Lacking her I cannot live.

> Dafydd ap Gwilym,
> *Cystudd y Bardd*,
> translated by Joseph P. Clancy.

96.

There left today superbly
The guard of generous Rhys,
Sworn brothers, foster brothers
And cousins, my yearning's keen,
Of mine, to trade blows with France—
From the South, Mary, speed them—
Proud hawks of the battle's breach,
Leaders of combat's brothers . . .

> Dafydd ap Gwilym,
> *A Wish for Eiddig (I Ddymuno Boddi'r Gŵr Eiddig)*,
> translated by Joseph P. Clancy.

In apt self-irony Dafydd styles himself *ddrychiolaeth hiraethlawn*, an "apparition full of longing," rather than *ddyn mewn agwedd iawn*," a man in good shape" :

I ddrychiolaeth hiraethlawn
Nog i ddyn mewn agwedd iawn.

> Dafydd ap Gwilym,
> *Ei Gysgod (The Shadow)*.

XVIII HIRAETH FOR THE MYTHIC AND LEGENDARY PAST

Hiraeth is not confined to personal losses of beloved places, people and things. The Welsh have a strong historic sense, and can feel the love-loss-longing syndrome for the ancestors and heroes of the race, and even beyond that, for symbolic, mythic and legendary matter embedded in the culture.

97.

The lost valley, with its tribe of lost Welsh [Fishlock is speaking about a recent search for an Arabic tribe reputed to speak Welsh], is a potent and enduring part of Welsh wistfulness and it fits quite naturally into the legends, folklore and history of a people who can look down the centuries as if down a mere staircase, who have their own private emotion called *hiraeth*, which is a kind of powerful nostalgic longing, against which a siren's song is but a television jingle, and who have for many years travelled and settled in the earth's imagined corners, setting up St. David's societies and Cambrian clubs and other Cymrodoric columns in many strange places. Myths and legends and dreams are important property, part of the constituent of a nation's soul.

Trevor Fishlock,
Talking of Wales.

98.

If we could free ourselves, yes, if only we could, from the fear, from the fright, from the nightmare of our world—but almost everyone is an enemy, we are weak, and it is enough today that we can remember the grief of the summer's going and enjoy the *hiraeth* of Branwen.

Alun Llywelyn-Williams,
Pe Bai'r Glaw yn Peidio (*If the Rain Stopped*),
translated by Gwynn ap Gwilym.

99. REMEMBERING

One short minute before the sun goes from the sky,
One gentle minute before the night starts on its journey,
To remember the forgotten things
Lost now in the dust of times gone by.

Like the foam of a wave that breaks on a lonely shore,
Like the wind's song where there is no ear to hear,
I know they call in vain upon us—
The old forgotten things of human kind.

The achievement and art of early generations,
Small dwellings and great halls,
The fine-wrought legends scattered centuries ago,
The gods that no one knows about by now.

And the little words of transient languages,
They were gay on the lips of men,
And pleasant to the ear in the chatter of little children,
But no tongue calls upon them any longer.

Oh, unnumbered generations of earth,
And their divine dreams and brittle divinity,
Does nothing but silence remain to the hearts
Which used to rejoice and grieve?

Often in the evening, when I am alone,
A longing comes to know you every one:
Is there anything which can keep you still in Heart and
Memory,
The old forgotten things of the human family?

Waldo Williams (1904-1971),
Cofio,
translated by R. Gerallt Jones.

Mynych ym mrig yr hwyr, a mi yn unig,
Daw hiraeth am eich 'nabod chwi bob un;
A oes a'ch deil o hyd mewn Cof a Chalon,
Hen bethau anghofiedig teulu dyn?

100. THE THREE DOVES

(In memory of T. Gwynn Jones)

The last thing today I saw them—thrilled by the sight of them—birds from magic regions of dreams, three swift ones flying to woods beyond all travail.

The very first gentle one is an image from the magic realm of ideals, and whitely it flows in the strength and wealth of Afallon and the leaves of its trees of balm.

There was no trace of age or affliction upon her, nor any trace of complaint or the bed of pain, and the soul, having seen her growth and watched her journey, will itself walk in its path.

It turned, clear above our country's wretchedness, and a long night in her history gathered throughout the borders of our language.

The second who strode in strength through the sky was beauty.

She does not linger for hiraeth inspires her wings.

She hurries to the ancient light of Broseliawnd—a realm of crystal plenty, of ages of beauty, a realm of peace and magic enclosed by groves, a realm of woods and lovely lakes.

While withdrawal keeps in memory the heart's pain, her wing will not fail nor be flaccid to please her.

The growth of the third bird was an image of the form and colour of sustenance.

No doubt it flies to the sun's house, in shame that the sunshine is prevented by the angry fog of our streets from benefitting a blameless hearth.

It flashed like a rending past, from the reaping of the field of grief and revenge in the world, past the desire of the harvest where Madog was drowned, on its leap from the earth to the place where the fire is unfailing nourishment, over the forms of the separating sea to walk the plains of Paradise.

And watching, I saw them in the sky's peace blending into one great-spirited flying being—Cynddilig of the forests, and the spiritual bond between him and the doves.

And the spiritual bond with the doves will bear us up in spite of his mute departure.

Euros Bowen,
Y Tair Colomen,
translated by R. Gerallt Jones.

Y TAIR COLOMEN

(Coffa am T. Gwynn Jones)

Heddiw'r peth diwethaf fe'u gwelais, yn gynnwrf o'u golwg,—adar o froydd hud ar freuddwydion, tair buain a hedai i wigoedd y tu hwnt i'r boenedigaeth:

Delw o fro hud delfrydiaeth yw y fwyn gyntaf un, a gwyn y dylifai o allu ac anadl Afallon a dail ei choed eli.

Nid oedd ôl haint na henaint arni hi, nac ôl cwyn na gwely cyni, ac o weld ei thwf a gwylied ei thaith, âi'r enaid i'w llwybr ei hunan.

Troai'n glir uwch trueni'n gwlad, a nos hir yn hanes hon yn crynhoi ar hyd cyrrau ein hiaith.

Harddwch oedd yr ail a gerddai'n rhywiog trwy'r awyr.

Nid erys am fod ei hiraeth yn donio ei hadenydd.

Brysiai i wawl hen Broséliawnd,—bro o risial lawnder, bro oesau o lendid, bro cau hud a hedd gan lwyni, bro coedydd a gwyn lynnoedd.

Cyhyd ag y bo encilio yn cadw i go boen calon, ni bydd i'w boddio na ffaeledig na phŵl ei hadain.

Llun o wedd a lliw nodded a oedd i dw'r trydydd aderyn.

Diau yr hed i dŷ yr haul, o gywilydd am gau heulwen gan niwl dig ein heolydd oddi wrth elw ar ddiwarth aelwyd.

Heibio fel rhwyg y gwibiai o fedel maes dolef a dial ym myd, heibio i ddihewyd y medi lle boddwyd Madog, ar ei llam o'r tir i'r lle mae'r tân yn faeth heb fethu, dros weddau y gwahanfor i droedio rhosydd Gwynfa.

Ac o wylio fe'u gwelwn yn hedd y nen yn toddi'n un eneidfawr yn hedfan,—Cynddilig y coedwigoedd a'r cwlwm enaid rhyngddo a'r colomennod.

A'r cwlwm enaid â'r colomennod a'n deil ar ei fudo ef.

(N.B. T. Gwynn Jones was a poet who drew much on mythological sources.)

XIX HIRAETH IN THE BONE

And sometimes *hiraeth* is a deep, almost instinctive feeling
for a lost meaning, or for roots reaching back into darkness,
or an indefinable longing, as though for lost things stored in
the racial memory.

101. PONIES, TWYNYRODYN

Winter, the old drover, has brought
these beasts from the high moor's hafod
to bide the bitter spell among us,
here, in the valley streets.
Observe them, this chill morning, as
they stand, backsides against the wind,
in Trevithick Row.
            Hoofs, shod with ice,
shift and clatter on the stone kerb.
Steam is slavering from red nostrils,
manes are stiff with frost and dung.

Quiet now, last night
they gallivanted through the village,
fear's bit in teeth. Hedges were broken,
there was havoc to parked cars. Yet,
despite the borough council's by-laws,
these refugees are welcome here.
Fed from kitchen and tommybox, they
are free to roam the grit backlanes,
only kids and mongrels pester them.
We greet them as old acquaintances
not because they bring us local colour,
as the tourist guides might say, but
for the brute glamour that is with them.
Long before fences and tarmac, they
were the first tenants of these valleys,
their right to be here is freehold.

Now, in this turncoat weather, as
they lord it through the long terraces,
toppling bins from wet steps, ribs
rubbing against the bent railings,
our smooth blood is disturbed
by hiraeth for the lost cantrefi,
the green parishes that lie beyond
the borders of our town and hearts,
fit for nothing now but sad songs.

These beasts are our companions,
dark presences from the peasant past,
these grim valleys our common hendre,
exiles all, until the coming thaw.

Meic Stephens.

This inchoate mystical inner sense is sometimes projected outwards onto the Macrocosm.

102.   THERE IS HIRAETH IN THE SEA

There is *hiraeth* in the sea and in the rambling hills, there is *hiraeth* in the silence and in song, in the murmuring of waters on their eternal journey, in the hours of sunset and in the flames of the fire; but most gently it complains in the wind, and it is in the sedges that the wind complains most sadly, awakening in the rushes echoes of old echoes, and memories of old memories in the heart. As when one listens in the long dawn to the cry of the cockerel on the gate close by, rousing song after clear song from the adjoining gardens, until yonder on the slopes a last cockerel picks up his cry with the sad gentleness of distant places in his voice.

R. Williams Parry (1884-1956),
Mae Hiraeth yn y Môr,
translated by Gwynn ap Gwilym.

XX HIRAETH FOR A HEROIC OR GOLDEN AGE

The Welshman's ever-present sense of history impels still other forms of *hiraeth*, not the least of which is an unrelievable ache for the passing of a proud social order, a Golden Age when Welsh culture was in full bloom.

Such was the *hiraeth* which led to the hope that the Welsh-born Henry Tudor, later Henry VII, would restore to Wales its rightful status—a hope that was dashed by the Act of Union of 1536.

103.
> There is longing for Harry,
> There is hope for our language.
>
> > Y mae hiraeth am Harri,
> > Y mae gobaith i'n hiaith.
>
> Robin Ddu (16th century).

104. THE REMAINDER

> They are the brave remainder that love her in her poverty,
> And who will stand in her support in the weary days;
> Out in the valleys and the patient mountains
> They face the alien wind and all weather.
>
> And they are the worthy remainder that see behind the
> unquiet rags
> In that black, rapacious wind
> The flowering of days before the pain of her scars;
> Those who in the last days pledged their souls for her
> With fire in their challenge, and her old hiraeth in their
> language.
>
> J. M. Edwards,
> *Y Gweddill*,
> translated by R. Gerallt Jones.

Hwynt-hwy ydyw'r gweddill dewr a'i câr yn ei thlodi,
Ac a saif iddi'n blaid yn ei dyddiau blin;
Allan yn y cymoedd a'r mynyddoedd amyneddgar
Hwy a wynebant yr estronwynt a phob hin.

A hwy ydyw'r gweddill da a wêl trwy ei charpiau
Aflonydd yn y gwynt du hwnnw a'i raib
Degwch blodeuog ei dydd cyn difwynder cur craith;
Y rhai yn y dyddiau diwethaf a blediodd eu henaid
                                                    drosti
Â thân yn eu her, a'i hen hiraeth hi yn eu hiaith.

105. LANGUAGE PROTEST, LLANGEFNI

It isn't even dramatic
Two shivering boys
Stood on a broad, flat roof,
The police themselves
Don't bother to force the issue.

They are free to come
Or to go:
We burn no martyrs
(For all of it's done in our name)
But learnt from Casement
How to discredit heroes—

The quiet whisper
"Iwan's a petty thief".
The glib assumption
Their cause is a mere insanity, their love
A strait-jacket passion
For out-dated gods.

Those two young boys,
Misguided perhaps, won't find
Anything more than a moment slipped between
Ulster and Africa:
Won't rot in an English gaol
For their love's persistence—
May find in an English lodging
Their only home.

Plaster the hills with hiraeth,
The roads with sign-posts
Fully approved, bilingual—
But also, first,
Make sure that those signs don't point
Forever east.

Sally Roberts Jones.

106. ARGOED

(Argoed represents a Celtic country in the early centuries
after Christ, threatened with Roman domination. It prefers
self-extinction to submission to a foreign power. The poem
captures the ideal, heroic society, and the *hiraeth* felt for the
loss of that ancient and noble order.)

I

Argoed, Argoed of the secret places . . .
Your hills, your sunken glades, where were they,
Your winding glooms and quiet towns?

Ah, quiet then, till doom was dealt you,
But after it, nothing save a black desert
Of ashes was seen of wide-wooded Argoed.

Argoed wide-wooded . . . Though you have vanished,
Yet from the unremembering depths, for a moment,
Is it there, your whispering ghost, when we listen—

Listen in silence to the wordless speech
Where the wave of yearning clings to your name,
Argoed, Argoed of the secret places?

II

. . .

Time out of mind the Children of Arofan
Had sustained their state purely, and never forsaken
The life of blessedness their fathers had known—
Hunting or herding, as there was need of it,
Living and suffering, as life required them,

91

Fearing no weakness, craving no luxuries,
Nor sought to oppress, nor feared the oppressor;
In such tranquility, generation to generation,
They raised strong sons and lovely daughters;
Recited their tales of courage of old times,
Attentative to hear, to know the true sentence
Of words of wisdom of men that were good men
And all the mysteries hidden in musecraft;
They listened to the secret learning of Druids,
Men with the gods themselves acquainted,
Who kept in the mind, generation to generation,
A wisdom of wonder-lore, not proper to be graved
On stone or wood, or preserved in writing.

Oh, then, how joyous were the days
In the quiet, mysterious forests of Argoed!
But she, in her ancient piety, knew not
Gaul was pulled down, under heel of her enemies,
And already the fame of her cities had dwindled
With coming of trickery, foreigner's ways,
To tame her energy, waste an old language
And custom as old as her earliest dawn.

. . .

IV

And tribute from Argoed was decreed, three times,
And then, three times, Argoed refused it,
For never had Argoed at all given honour
To a foreign might or brutal oppression;
The heart of her people kept faith; richness
Of her history had not lapsed to oblivion;
And none but the vilest among them would suffer
An enemy's yoke without wincing in shame,
Or bear, without blushing, its naked disgrace.

' We'll not give tribute, let forests be fired first,
Let the last of the Children of Arofan die,
Nor mock our past, nor forswear an old language,
Nor custom as old as our earliest dawn! '

To the bounds of Argoed quickly the word went,
Each of her citizens was constant and sure;
The doom was pronounced, without one to cross it,
The course was ventured, no man flinched from it;
For all his trickery, no foreigner had tribute,
Chattel nor booty, nor man to be beaten;
Nothing was found there, or only a wasteland,
Desolation of ashes, where once were wide woods.

V

. . .

Argoed, wide-wooded . . . Though you have vanished,
Yet from the unremembering depths, for a moment,
Are you there, unconquerable soul, when we listen—

Listen in silence to the wordless speech
Where the wave of yearning clings to your name,
Argoed, Argoed of the secret places?

T. Gwynn Jones (1871-1949),
Argoed,
translated by Anthony Conran.

Too often such *hiraeth* is already tinged with the feeling that the wish is forlorn. Yet to be *di-hiraeth*—without the capacity to regret and lament, to be, in short, blunted, insensitive and indifferent—is a far worse condition of the human spirit than the anguish of grief.

The following line comes from a poem, *Cymru*, *1937*, in which the poet, R. Williams Parry exhorts the Wind to shake up the world and restore to human beings the best qualities of humanness, including caring and sensitivity:

Bedyddia'r di-hiraeth a'th ddagrau, a'r doeth ailgristia;
Baptise the insensitive (those without *hiraeth*) with your tears and rechristen the wise.

In a poem of regret for those voices "that have strayed from their ancient homage", that have lost the Welsh language, the poet pities them most for their experiencing no *hiraeth* for their loss:

107.
But there is a country where the lark no longer climbs sky-
                                                                         wards;
Some unlamented yesterday has separated them.
This is the winter of a nation, the cold heart
Which does not know it has lost its five joys.

Waldo Williams, (1904-1971)
Yr Heniaith (*The Old Language*),
translated by R. Gerallt Jones.

Ond mae tir ni ddring ehedydd yn ôl i'w nen;
Rhyw ddoe dihiraeth a'u gwahanodd.
Hyn yw gaeaf cenedl, y galon oer
Heb wybod colli ei phum llawenydd.

To yearn in vain is far better than not to yearn at all. Forlorn *hiraeth*, akin to what Yeats has called "tragic joy", a mustering of courage in the face of impossible odds, is the source of much of the poignancy in Celtic literature noted by many scholars.

108.

Thus the Celtic race has worn itself out in resistance to its time, and in the defence of desperate causes . . .

Thence ensues its sadness. Take the songs of its bards of the sixth century; they weep more defeats than they sing victories. Its history is itself only one long lament; it still recalls its exiles, its flights across the seas. If at times it seems to be cheerful, a tear is not slow to glisten behind its smile; it does not know that strange forgetfulness of human conditions and destinies which is called gaiety. Its songs of joy end as elegies; there is nothing to equal the delicious sadness of its national melodies. One might call them emanations from on high which, falling drop by drop upon the soul, pass through it like memories of another world. Never have men feasted so long upon these solitary delights of the spirit, these poetic memories which simultaneously intercross all the sensations of life, so vague, so deep, so penetrative, that one might die from them, without being able to say whether it was from bitterness or sweetness.

Ernest Renan (19th century),
The Poetry of the Celtic Races.

109.

The Celts, with their vehement reaction against the despotism of fact, with their sensuous nature, their manifold striving, their adverse destiny, their immense calamities, the Celts are the prime authors of the vein of piercing regret and passion—of this Titanism in poetry.

Matthew Arnold (19th century),
On the Study of Celtic Literature.

Such forlornness may be for a lack which is absolutely unattainable or a loss that is irretrievable:

95

110.

> . . . We do find, constantly recurring, a note of *hiraeth*, that typically Welsh word which we can but inadequately render as ' longing ': an intense, passionate yearning for that which we have not, for dead friends, vanished youth, the peace of Heaven, some satisfaction which life can never give.

H. Idris Bell (1879-1976),
The Development of Welsh Poetry.

111.

Snow on the mountain, fish in the ford
the thin bowed stag seeks the snug valley;
longing for a dead one brings no joy.

Gnomic verse (pre-12th century),
from the *Red Book of Hergest*,
translated by Gwyn Williams.

Eiry mynyd pysc ynryt
kyrchyt carw culgrwm cwm clyt,
hiraeth am varw ny weryt.

112. COED GLYN CYNON—The Wood of Glyn Cynon

In Aberdâr and all Llanwynno, in the parish of Merthyr as far as Llanfabon, there was never more adversity than when the woods of Glyn Cynon were felled.

Many a sweet grove where men and youths met in the days of good Queen Bess has been cut down. Glyn Cynon was so serene.

If there was ever a man on the run before foreigners, the nightingale would always shelter him in the woods of Glyn Cynon.

And if she of the fair countenance ever came to stroll along the banks of the river, she would find a pleasant place for a tryst in the woods of Glyn Cynon.

Many a green mantled birch (may the English be hanged for it) is now blazing in the fires of the black men of the iron-works.

Llanbadarn Fawr, Aberystwyth, Dyfed.

Pembroke Town and Castle, Dyfed.

It would be better if the English were hanged and thrown to the bottom of the sea to maintain their mansions in hell's tortures than that they should have cut the green trees of Glyn Cynon.

I vow that I have heard it said that a herd of red deer are leaving their old haunts in desperation. They have left for the dark forests of Mawddwy.

No more will there be any chasing of wild boar, or hunting the stag from the woody hills. It is in vain that one pursues the hind, now that the woods of Glyn Cynon have been felled.

I insist on summoning those responsible to be tried by the honest birds, and I shall call the owl to be hangman.

If anyone should ask who made this song of cruel sorrow, he is a man who once kept a love-tryst in the woods of Cynon.

Anonymous (16th century),
translated by Gwynn ap Gwilym.

113.

An old man in Powys burdened by necessity, the ill-fated, without habitation shepherding his loneliness, and the fruit of his body wounding the ford, food to the red beak and the talon. Time that was has gone.

Gwyn Thomas,
Cwestiwn,
translated by R. Gerallt Jones.

(The old man is Llywarch the Old)

Hen ŵr ym Mhowys dan ei raid, y diriaid,
Heb gyfannedd yn bugeilio 'i hiraeth,
A ffrwyth ei gnawd yn clwyfo'r rhyd, yn faeth
I'r ylfin goch a'r grafanc. Amser a fu, a aeth.

XXII   HIRAETH FOR YOUTH

No *hiraeth* is more forlorn than pining for lost youth.

114.

Hiraeth am mebyd ni weryd

Longing for youth will not avail.

Proverb

115. SENTENCES WHILE REMEMBERING HIRAETHOG

it was a summer evening
they were all there
o I remember them I tell you

old people that are this scorching hour
no more than tattered lips in the wind
and the others
the red-ripe hearts
with their laughter in fragments amongst the reeds
and their hair unkempt

where are the buttermilk voices that used to flow
through the kitchen and the dairy and the cowshed

and the laughter in fragments among the reeds

where are the round eyes
that disappeared in a cloud of laughter

I prayed that I might be one of the colts
on the Oerfa mountain for ever
it would be damned cold in winter of course
said Jo laughingly
odd that his voice that minute was like a bell

It was a summer evening
they were all there
the wind idly meandered through the corn

oh I remember them I tell you.

T. Glynne Davies,
Brawddegau wrth Gofio Hiraethog,
translated by R. Gerallt Jones.

116. AN AGE

The blue singleness of summer was in that air
And the bushes hazed after the light
Though it was September gone.
Is it blackberrying, sun
And juice in the hand, or a flight
Of birds shearing over the ferry that holds me there?

The envelope has let an age escape to the sea
And I am old, but not so
Old as Mabon taken from between
His mother and the wall. When
I was young I saw the sun go
Purple on my thumb and birds stand shoaling in the estuary.

Roland Mathias.

117. WATERFALLS

Always in that valley in Wales I hear the noise
    Of waters falling.
                        There is a clump of trees
        We climbed for nuts; and high in the trees the boys
            Lost in the rookery's cries
                Would cross, and branches cracking under their
                                                    knees

Would break, and make in the winter wood new gaps.
  The leafmould covering the ground was almost black,
    But speckled and striped were the nuts we threw in our
      caps,
        Milked from split shells and cups,
          Secret as chestnuts when they are tipped from a
            sack,

Glossy and new.
                    Always in that valley in Wales
  I hear that sound, those voices. They keep fresh
    What ripens, falls, drops into darkness, fails,
      Gone when dawn shines on scales,
        And glides from village memory, slips through the
          mesh,

And is not, when we come again.
                              I look:
  Voices are under the bridge, and that voice calls,
    Now late, and answers;
                          then, as the light twigs break
      Back, there is only the brook
        Reminding the stones where, under a breath, it
          falls.

                              Vernon Watkins (1906-1967),

XXIII   HIRAETH WITHOUT HOPE

Forlorn *hiraeth* can modulate into hopelessness, and thence
into ultimate desolation, and despair.

118. THE BARD'S LAST CYWYDD

> To think of my lost young days, this is my sorrow,
> Keening deep to my heart like a flighting arrow.
> I cry to my Lord to raise me, to succour me,
>   O weary must be my days!
> Sure to its grave youth flieth and is gone;
> If it was brave, now are the brave days done;
> My thoughts have dying ways, but though all die
>   Still love revenging stays.
>
> Cast from my lips afar is the spirit of song,
> Music of joy, my living delight so long.
> Ifor, my wisdom, where is he with his fame?
> Or Nest, my refuge, his noble and fair young dame?
> Where in the woods is Morvyth, my darling fled?
>   They all lie dead in the mould.
> But here I linger, old and in heaviness
> Bearing my woeful burden of cold distress.
>
> No more I sing, nor try what should be sweet
> Of the wild wood, the vetch or tares in the wheat;
> I hope no more of the gleaming woodland dale,
> Cuckoo at dawn, dusk or the nightingale,
> Nor yet a kiss of my love, nor speech of hers;
> She neither speaks, poor tender child, nor stirs.
>
> A spear-thrust in my breast is old, old age,
> Love of fair women leaves for heritage
> That, that still wounds which no balm can assuage,
>   Sorrow to think on now.
> My strength ebbs fast, like chaff before the wind
> It fleeth, nor can death wait far behind,
>   Ghostly and pale of brow.

The grave makes ready. When at Thy last command
Trembling before thee, O Lord Christ I stand—
Son of sweet Mary, O be thou my stay,
    Be merciful that day.

Dafydd ap Gwilym, (16th century),
Y Cywydd Diweddaf,
translated by Robert Gurney.

119. DE PROFUNDIS

Strait, strait and narrow is the vale!
Behind me riseth to the skies
What I have been: in front, but dim,
What I shall be all shrouded lies,
All shrouded by the curtain dark
Of mists which from the river rise.
Above, the clouds hide from mine eyes
The hosts of heaven.

Strait, strait and barren is the vale!
For here no tender primrose blows,
Nor daisy with its simple charm,
Nor from the yews which round me close
Comes song of thrush—but dismal shriek
Of deathbird, scattering as it goes
The stillness deep—and pales my cheek
With awe unspeakable.

Strait, strait and lonely is the vale!
Only from far falls on my ear
The murmur of the world I loved,
But death's dark torrent roareth near.
Now 'neath my feet the path I tread
Crumbling gives way, and filled with dread
Into the waves below I hear
The fragments falling.

Strait, strait and hopeless is the vale!
Nor can I evermore regain
The days of happiness and health
Which once I knew, days free from pain,

Nor move a foot from where I stand,
And backward eyes of longing strain
A moment—ere I leave the land
And brave the waters.

Yet strait tho' be the vale and dim,
And though the skies are dark and drear,
And though the mountains everywhere
Rise steep and rugged round me here
To bar me out from life ! there lives
One Star which shineth bright and clear
From out the sky and comfort gives
To soothe my sadness.

> Robert Owen, who was already dying of
> consumption when he emigrated to Australia,
> Translated by Edmund O. Jones.

120. MY COUNTRY, MY GRIEF

Anguish is my country.
I would not recognize
A land where only fair winds blow
And the sun shines.

But the land where every wind
Is the breath of guilt
Is home, and let the loud seas lash
Wherever I have slept.

My paradise will be despair
And the cold winds that blow
About the rocks, about your hair
And the grief I know.

> T. Harri Jones (1921-1965),

DIFFERENCE

Under God's violent unsleeping eye
My fathers laboured for three hundred year;
On the same farm, in the expected legend.
Their hymns were anodynes against defeat,
But sin, the original and withering worm,
Was always with them, whether they excelled
In prayers, made songs on winter nights,
Or slobbered in temptation, women, drink.

I inherit their long arms and mountain face,
The withering worm sleeps too within my blood
But I know loneliness, unwatched by God.

T. Harri Jones,

122. GWLADYS RHYS

Seiat, Prayer Meeting, Dorcas, Children's Meeting;
my father all day and night as cross as the wind,
and the wind all day and night in the pine branches
around the minister's house. And my mother,
trying to learn the language of heaven, with no language
but talk of services, Seiat, Meeting and Dorcas.

What was there for me to do, Gwladys Rhys,
eldest daughter of the Reverend Thomas Prys,
pastor of Horeb, on the Rhos? What besides
much bitter yearning, turning miserably
my eyes hither and hither across the meadow,
getting up in the morning to long for night,
tossing through the long night in expectation of morning?
And winter, o my God, drawing the curtains
across the windows at four in the afternoon,
hearing the wind complain in the pine branches
and listening to my parents' conversation!

One day there came Someone towards the house
and I felt something strange in my heart:
there was no wind complaining in the pines,
there was no longer any need for my eyes
to turn back and forth over the meadow. A gust
of some sweet breeze came from the far horizons.

Over the window then I drew the curtain,
not answering my father's cold bad temper
or listening to my mother's lengthy tale
of the Daughters of Gwynedd Temperance Society:
with no word to anyone I went out through the snow,
when the wind was complaining through the pines
and the evening was that of the Seiat and Dorcas Meeting.

It's for that reason, traveller, that I lie
near Horeb Chapel—Gwladys Rhys,
thirty years old, and mother and father
pass by me to the Seiat and the service,
the Prayer Meeting, Dorcas, and committees
of the Daughters of Gwynedd Temperance Society,
here in the valley of forgetfulness, because the gust
I once felt coming from the far horizons
was only the sound of the wind complaining in the pines.

W. J. Gruffydd (1881-1954),
translated by Gwyn Williams.

XXIV   HIRAETH AND THE QUEST FOR THE IDEAL

At least until recent times, a prodigious hopefulness counter-balanced the *hiraeth* of forlornness and desolation. Just as there seems to be a perpetual tension in the Welsh between an urge to stay and an urge to leave, a desire for roots and a desire for wings, so there is a forward-looking optimistic yearning off-setting the pessimism just considered.

123.

> Imaginative power is nearly always proportionate to the concentration of feeling, and lack of the external development of life . . . Compared with the classical imagination, the Celtic imagination is indeed the infinite contrasted with the finite . . . The essential element in the Celt's poetic life is the *adventure*—that is to say the pursuit of the unknown, an endless quest after an object ever flying from desire . . . This race desires the infinite, it thirsts for it, and pursues it at all costs, beyond the tomb, beyond hell itself . . . Thence arises the profound sense of the future and of the eternal destinies of his race, which has ever borne up the Cymry, and kept him young still beside his conquerors who have grown old. Thence that dogma of the resurrection of the heroes . . . Thence *Celtic Messianism*, that belief in a future avenger who shall restore Cambria, and deliver her out of the hands of her oppressors . . . It is thus that little people dowered with imagination revenge themselves on their conquerors. Feeling themselves to be strong inwardly and weak out-wardly, they protest, they exult; and such a strife unloosing their might, renders them capable of miracles. Nearly all great appeals to the supernatural are due to people hoping against all hope . . .
>
> Few heroes owe less to reality than Arthur . . . It was by this ideal and representative character that the Arthurian legend had such an astonishing prestige throughout the whole world . . . How otherwise shall we explain why a forgotten tribe on the very confines of the world should have

imposed its heroes upon Europe, and, in the domain of imagination, accomplished one of the most singular revolutions known to the historian of letters? . . . A new element entered into the poetic conception of the Christian peoples, and modified it profoundly.

Ernest Renan (19th century),
The poetry of the Celtic Races.

124. THE BIRDS OF RHIANNON

The birds of Rhiannon are fervent, unseen,
hurt by the ill-luck of our heroes;
there comes from the grief of the harp
a gentle weeping for the land of apples.

The land of apples gave abundant homes
with the joy of orchards,
till the trampling of good under the terror
of stallions, the power impelling them
a wintry grip.

From winter on a thousand fields,
from old roots we'll see early goodness,
energy will rise with the joy
of stallions, the power impelling them
like a sprouting in the grip of spring.

The birds of Rhiannon, fervently greeting,
love the renown of heroes:
surely the harp's calling
will bring back summer to the land of apples.

Euros Bowen,
Adar Rhiannon,
translated by Gwyn Williams.

125. FREE WALES

And yet I sing my country,
for Wales shall one day be
the happiest and loveliest land,
a time when we will see
no violent hand to waste her,
no coward to betray her,
no quarrelling to weaken her
and then Wales shall be free.

Sir John Morris-Jones (1864-1929),
Cymru Rydd.

126.

Wales has also had a toilsome march. It has traversed
many a mountain and marsh: it has been attacked by in-
numerable foes: and the national existence of this brave
little army of patriots appeared many a time to have been
blotted out. But it has surmounted every obstacle; it has
crossed every steep hill and morass; it has vanquished the
efforts of every enemy by the indomitable vitality of its
patriotism. It has a few more battles to fight, but Wales will
not turn back, for beneath lie the fruit-laden valleys of the
future and the golden gates of Cymru Fydd.

Rt. Hon. David Lloyd George, from a speech at
Liverpool, November 20, 1891.

127.

Emrys Wledig :   A vineyard given to my care
is Wales my country,
to pass on to my children
and to my children's children
an everlasting heritage.

Saunders Lewis,
Buchedd Garmon,
translated by Gwyn Williams.

XXV ANTI-HIRAETH, IRONIC HIRAETH, AND A NEW REALISTIC HIRAETH

Wales had not been impervious to the twentieth-century spirit of scepticism, however. Some of the comrades believe that redemption cannot come from these wide swings between hope and despair, nor from a sentimental fixation on the past on the one hand, and an impossible ideal on the other. By asking for a realistic appraisal of the present, these advocates of "anti-*hiraeth*"—of the rejection of old brands of *hiraeth*—are actually expressing a new form of *hiraeth* for more readily attainable goals. An essential element of this new attitude is self-irony, even mockery—a timely reminder not to take ourselves too seriously lest our best traits disappear.

128. APOLOGIA

Your Wales was never mine, I know.
The towering shadows the dead throw
lie like elegies over your day.
I usually face the other way.
For you the present is the last
dying moment of the past.
For me the present is the first
leaf-green bud from which will burst
the future, like an un-named rose
for my children's hands to close
themselves around, bend to and breathe:
the flowering Wales that you bequeath.

Raymond Garlick.

129. A WELSH WORDSCAPE

1. To live in Wales,

   Is to be mumbled at
   by re-incarnation of Dylan Thomas
   in numerous diverse disguises.

Is to be mown down
by the same words
at least six times a week.

Is to be bored
by Welsh visionaries
with wild hair and grey suits.

It is to be told
of the incredible agony
of an exile
that can be at most
a days travel away.

And the sheep, the sheep,
the bloody flea-bitten Welsh sheep,
chased over the same hills
by a thousand poetic phrases
all saying the same thing.

To live in Wales
is to love sheep
and to be afraid
of dragons.

2. A history is being re-lived
    a lost heritage
    is being wept after
    with sad eyes and dry tears.

    A heritage
    that spoke beauty to the world
    through dirty fingernails
    and endless alcoholic mists.

    A heritage
    that screamed that once,
    that exploded that one holy time
    and connected Wales
    with the whirlpool
    of the universe.

A heritage
that ceased communication
upon a death, and nonetheless
tried to go on living.

A heritage
that is taking
a long time to learn
that yesterday cannot be today
and that the world
is fast becoming bored
with language forever
in the same tone of voice.

Look at the Welsh landscape,
look closely,
new voices must rise,
for Wales cannot endlessly remain
chasing sheep into the twilight.

Peter Finch.

130.   WELSH LANDSCAPE

To live in Wales is to be conscious
At dusk of the spilled blood
That went to the making of the wild sky,
Dyeing the immaculate rivers
In all their courses.
It is to be aware,
Above the noisy tractor
And hum of the machine
Of strife in the strung woods,
Vibrant with sped arrows.
You cannot live in the present,
At least not in Wales.
There is the language for instance,
The soft consonants
Strange to the ear.
There are cries in the dark at night
As owls answer the moon,

And thick ambush of shadows,
Hushed at the fields' corners.
There is no present in Wales,
And no future;
There is only the past,
Brittle with relics,
Wind-bitten towers and castles
With sham ghosts;
Mouldering quarries and mines;
And an impotent people,
Sick with inbreeding,
Worrying the carcase of an old song.

R. S. Thomas.

XXVI   SPIRITUAL AND RELIGIOUS HIRAETH

There is a form of forward-looking *hiraeth*, more personal than social, which continues to give heart to many Welsh people wherever they may be found across the world. This is spiritual *hiraeth*, the yearning for an Ideal Homeland beyond the precincts of this world.

131.

When we come down to modern days, the note changes a little, the *hiraeth* becomes more spiritual, more religious, and in doing so acquires a deeper intensity . . .

When this note of wistfulness is united with the delicacy of conception and the power of bare, direct, seeming-effortless and infinitely significant expression which are other characteristic gifts of Welsh poetry the resulting verses are at times quite heartrending in their perfect simplicity . . .

The Celts are . . . eternal children . . . and in some of the Welsh poems we have a feeling that the author is looking with unacquainted eyes at a new world, coming for the first time, and with wondering incomprehension, into the presence of sorrow and death.

H. Idris Bell (1879-1967),
The Development of Welsh Poetry.

132.

After the sermon one of the prisoners would give out a hymn which would then be sung. The hymns chosen without fail were: "See above the clouds of time", "From the hills of Jerusalem", "The Golden Harp", "I long for the country",—the hymns of heaven. The singing was loud and passionate; the last verse was doubled and trebled and quadrupled as in the revival meetings in the time of the Reverend John Jones of Talsarn. Myrddin Tomos could not

113

but join in the spiritual *hiraeth* of the hymn for the land
beyond the veil . . .

D. Gwenallt Jones (1899-1968),
Plasau'r Brenin,
translated by Gwynn ap Gwilym.

133.

Hiraeth is in my heart
To get the beautiful taste
Of conquering the passions which till today
Went against heavenly grace;
This is the very lovely gift
That I am seeking morning and noon.

I see the high hills
Of precious deliverance;
Oh, that I might attain them
Before the afternoon sun goes down;
That is my cry toward heaven;
Gentle Jesus, hear it.

William Williams, Pantycelyn (1717-1791).

Y mae hiraeth yn fy nghalon
Am gael teimlo hyfryd flas
Concwest nwydau sydd hyd heddiw
Yn gwrthnebu'r nefol ras;
Dyma ddawn hyfryd iawn,
Wy'n ei 'mofyn fore a nawn.

'R wyf yn gweled bryniau uchel
Gwaredigaeth werthfawr, lawn;
O! na chawn i eu meddiannu
Cyn machludo, haul brynhawn;
Dyna'm llef tua'r nef;
Addfwyn Iesu, gwrando ef.

134.

I am standing on the stormy banks
of old black Jordan
Gazing gravely in sharp *hiraeth*
At Canaan's hills aloft.

Ieuan Glan Geirionydd (Evan Evans, 1795-1855),
translated by Gwen Watts Jones.

'Rwy'n sefyll ar dymhestlog lan
Yr hen Iorddonen ddu,
Gan syllu'n ddwys mewn hiraeth clau
Ar fryniau'r Ganaan fry.

Such *hiraeth* is not to be confused with routine religious experience, much less with lip service and hypocrisy.

135.

From his hospital bed shortly before his death the poet takes stock of the genuineness of his emotions throughout his life, and finds them to have been thespian and insincere much of the time. In the following lines he tells of putting on a big crying act at a prayer meeting on Rhys Defi's watchnight, for motives he now recognizes as a need to draw attention to himself in order not to be left out by those who were ex-eriencing the true *hiraeth* for redemption:

Neu a wyt ti'n gofio di'n bymtheg oed
yng nghwrdd gweddi gwylnos Rhys Defi ?
'Roedd llifogydd dy ddagrau di'n boddi hiraeth pawb
arall,—
("ar dorri 'i galon fach" medden' nhw, "druan bach")—
a llais dy wylofain di fel cloch dynnu sylw;
dim ond am fod hunandod hiraeth pobol eraill
yn bygwth dy orchuddio di, a'th gadw di y tu allan i'r
digwydd.

J. Kitchener Davies (1902-1952),
Swn y Gwynt sy'n Chwythu.

Welsh religious revivalism—largely a reaction to social, political and economic ills—produced many hymns of *hiraeth*, their fervour often reaching apocalyptic intensity.

136.   TREFALDWYN

Jesus, give me Thy heavenly company
   In this barren land
Where there are snares after snares
To confuse me constantly.
There is hiraeth in my heart,
   And signs without ebb
To see the hour of my deliverance
   Happy, fair, at hand.

William Williams, Pantycelyn (1717-1791),
translated by Gwen Watts Jones.

Iesu dyro dy gymdeithas
   Nefol yn yr anial fyd,
Lle mae maglau ar ôl maglau
   Yn fy nrysu 'mron o hyd;
Y mae hiraeth yn fy nghalon,
   Ac ochneidiau heb ddim trai,
Am weld oriau 'ngwaredigaeth
   Ddedwydd hyfryd yn nesau.

137.   MINFFORDD

Behold the region, behold the haven,
   Behold the heavenly land.
Behold the pure path made plain
   Which leads this hour to my Father's house.
There is hiraeth in my heart
   To be today in that celestial place,
With the myriad saints who are singing the anthem,
   The anthem of love—"To Him."

William Williams, Pantycelyn,
translated by Gwen Watts Jones.

Dacw'r ardal, dacw'r hafan,
   Dacw'r nefol hyfryd wlad,
Dacw'r llwybyr pur yn amlwg
   'R awron tua thŷ fy Nhad;
Y mae hiraeth yn fy nghalon
   Am fod heddiw draw yn nhref,
Gyda myrdd sy'n canu'r anthem,
   Anthem cariad, "Iddo Ef."

138. ST. BEUNO

Hiraeth is in my tender heart
   Of seeing the day
   That I'll be free
Of my pain and weariness.

William Williams, Pantycelyn,
translated by Gwen Watts Jones.

Hiraeth sy ar fy nghalon dyner
   Am weld dydd
   Mynd yn rhydd
Maes o'm poen a'm blinder.

139. Y NEFOEDD

My sorrowful heart is yearning
   To see those heavenly regions;
My God, my Christ, Oh my Father,
May I enter that glorious land
   To worship Thee in Heaven.

Ieuan Gwyllt (John Roberts, 1822-1877),
translated by Gwen Watts Jones.

Hiraethu mae fy nghalon drist
   Am weld y teg ardaloedd;
Fy Nuw, fy Iesu, O! fy Nhad,
A gaf fi ddod i'r hyfryd wlad,
   I'th foli yn y nefoedd?

140. RHEWL-HIR

I watch and wait continually,
And long for the dawn,
When I shall be free from sin,
And can cast down my burden
And awake to Thy image,
When I shall see Thy worthy face,
When I shall worship without ceasing,
And be forever like my God.

Rev. Thomas Charles of Bala (1755-1814),
translated by Gwen Watts Jones.

Edrych 'r wyf, a hynny beunydd,
A hiraethu am y wawr,
Pryd y derfydd im a phechod,
Ac y caf roi 'meichiau i lawr,
Y caf ddihuno ar dy ddelw,
Pan gaf weld dy wyneb gwiw,
Pan gaf foli byth heb dewi,
A bod yn debyg byth i'm Duw.

141. Y DDOL

Longing am I, God's gentle lamb,
For refuge in Thy worthy wounds,
And cleansing in Thy precious blood
Of all my sins, and finding freedom.

John Wesley: from English to German to English to Welsh,
translated from the Welsh by Gwen Watts Jones

Hiraethu'r wyf, Oen addfwyn Duw,
Am noddfa yn dy glwyfau gwiw,
A'm golchi yn dy werthfawr waed,
O'm pechod oll i gael rhyddhad.

Do not pass me by, gracious Saviour,
 I sicken for Thy companionship,
I yearn for Thy love,
 When Thou callest,
  Call me, yes, me,
 When Thou callest, call me.

Ieuan Gwyllt (1822-1877),
translated by Gwen Watts Jones.

Na ddos heibio, raslawn Geidwad,
 Claf wyf am dy gwmni Di;
Rwy'n hiraethu am Dy gariad,
 Pan yn galw, galw fi.
  Ie fi, ie fi,
 Pan yn galw, galw fi.

XXVIII HIRAETH FOR THE CELTIC OTHERWORLD

Spiritual *hiraeth* is mystical in the sense that the individual finds his own way to insight and illumination rather than relying on the experience and word of others. Often, elements of the Celtic Otherworld, the Land of Avalon in the Western Seas, are blended with the Christian vision of Paradise.

143.

Over the sea there is a gentle land in which grief does not tarry, nor does any pestilence or old age grip those who come to its pure, free breeze, and every heart there remains vigorous and happy. That is the Isle of Afallon.

In that happy land there are old dreams which have eased the fears of the ages; every ancient hope is still alive there, and high intentions flourish. There will never come to pollute this place any loss of faith nor any shameful deed nor any heartbreak.

The fire of every muse that sings is in that place; and the vigour, the confidence, the zest of every man who strives. It is ever a foundation for him who wishes to hope. It gives energy to him who wishes to reform. While it gives patronage we shall not grow old. There is fine morality in that place, and there too is the nation's breath of life.

T. Gwynn Jones (1871-1949),
Ymadawiad Arthur,
translated by Gwynn ap Gwilym.

144. SEE ABOVE THIS MORTAL CLOUDLAND

See, above this mortal cloudland,
O, my soul, the land appear
where the breeze is always gentle,
where the sky is always clear.
   Happy multitude,
  now floating in its peace.

Cardiff Castle and the River Taff.

Hafod Mansion, near Aberystwyth, Dyfed.

There the springs of life are welling,
there meander streams of peace,
watering its lovely regions
to a beauty not to cease;
    for salvation
  will be breathed upon its shores.

And death's arrows are not able
to its nearest part to rise,
and our mortal enemy dare not
tread this region of the skies.
    Home to live in!
  It is our immortal home!

For the breezes of death's valley
turn to peace beyond this door,
and the sighs of all homesickness
turn to anthems on this shore;
    the last tear
  into Jordan's blackness falls.

No one here has cause for weeping,
no one here knows misery;
wormwood here is turned to honey
and the captive is made free.
    Happy multitude,
  who will live there ever more!

My sad heart begins its leaping,
jubilating in my breast,
in the hope of now possessing
this divinely given bequest.
    Happy multitude,
  with its face towards the land.

                    Islwyn (William Thomas, 1832-1878),
                        Gwel Uwchlaw Cymylau Amser,
                        translated by Gwyn Williams.

Fourth stanza :

    Troir awelon glyn marwolaeth
    Oll yn hedd tu yma i'r fan,
    Try holl ocheneidiau hiraeth
    Yn anthemau ar y lan;
    Syrth y deigryn
    Olaf i'r Iorddonen ddu.

145. PRAYER

God will grant me love within heaven's walls
May I win from God after sinning
The bond of peace, land of paradise,
Where no man is older or younger,
Where comes no trouble, cloud of hardship
I pray God's favour at heaven's portals,
May Peter not set locks
To keep me from a place of my own;
Mine, my Father's house;

Einion ap Gwalchmai (13th century),
translated by Joseph P. Clancy.

146.

He saw the white homeland of Paradise
with its fair towers, its holy choir,
and the four rivers of sweet water
urgently running through it;
wine and milk, bright worthy mouths,
the song of faith, and honey and oil.

Rhys Goch Eryri (Red Rhys of Snowdon, 15th century),
from a poem in praise of St. Beuno,
translated by Gwyn Williams.

Gweles henwlad Baradwys
A'i chaerau glan a'i chor glwys,
A'r pedair afon, ton teg,
Rhydaer drwyddi yn rhedeg;
Gwin a llaeth, gwiw enau llew,
Mawl goel, a mel ac olew.

XXIX   HIRAETH AND PLATONIC
RECOLLECTION

For many Welsh people, spiritual *hiraeth* paradoxically looks
back as well as forward—to a state that the soul enjoyed before
it entered the vale of tears, and will resume again after the
body expires. The Platonic doctrine of Recollection and
Wordsworth's "Intimations of Immortality from Recollections
of Early Childhood" are of a piece with Vaughan's and Islwyn's
vision of return to an earlier Homeland of the soul.

147.   O how I long to travel back,
       And tread again that ancient track!
       That I might once more reach that plain
       Where first I left my glorious train;
       From whence th'enlightened spirit sees
       That shady City of Palm-trees.
       But ah! my soul with too much stay
       Is drunk, and staggers in the way!
       Some men a forward motion love,
       But I by backward steps would move;
       And when this dust falls to the urn,
       In that state I came, return.

Henry Vaughan (1621-1695),
The Retreat.

148.   . . . What mortal man lives now who never feels
       The sudden spin of a long forgotten world
       Flashing across his path, strangely familiar,
       Or brushing the tip of a long promontory
       Of memories? . . .
               . . . O blessed hour, when God
       Appears, a Sun in Majesty above
       Earth's many days, and the Holy Spirit's path
       A ray of light on the world's broken tracks
       Lighting the way back to those heights Divine!

Islwyn (1832-1878),
Intimations,
translated by D. M. Lloyd.

XXX   POETRY AND HIRAETH

Sufferers of hiraeth can seldom hope to find release through the restoration of beloved places, people, things or conditions that are lost from or lacking in their lives. Relief from pain ranging from gentle nostalgia to anguished longing and near-despair can be found only in the catharsis of expression. Hence *hiraeth* and poetry are inextricably linked in the Welsh literary tradition, as the many items in this volume demonstrate.

It was ever the bard's honoured function to praise to mourn, and to yearn :

149.
THE BARD'S FUNCTION IN THE HALL OF HIS PATRON

> After the Mass we go together
> to the well-timbered hall.
> I am caused to be placed
> correctly in this hall,
> to sit, when silence is proclaimed,
> fine custom, at high table.
> Gift for gift in its kind
> comes to my lord, for he is Nudd.
> Drink for drink comes to me
> from his vineyard, from his fair hand.
> From poetry, eloquent of longing,
> and music, we get glory.

> Iolo Goch (14th century),
> from a poem in praise of the Bishop of St. Asaph,
> translated by Gwyn Williams.

> Ar ôl Offeren yr awn
> i'r neuadd gydladd goedlawn.
> Peri fy rhoddi ar radd
> iawn a wnai yn y neuadd,
> i eistedd fry ar osteg
> ar y ford dal, arfer teg.

Anrheg am anrheg unrhyw
a ddoi i'r arglwydd, Nudd yw.
Diod am ddiod a ddaw
o'i winllan im o'i wenllaw.
Cerdd dafawd ffraeth hiraethlawn,
cerdd dant, gogoniant a gawn.

After battle, it was the bard's priestly function to sing the
praises of the slain and mourn their loss, while the survivors
passed the *hirlas*, the ceremonial drinking horn, in a ritual
expression of their *hiraeth*.

150.   Menestr a'm gorthaw, na'm adawed,
As deuy â'r corn, er cydyfed,
Hiraethlawn, amliw, lliw ton nawfed,
Hirlas ei arwydd, aur ei dudded.

Cup-bearer, what stills me, may it stay mine,
Bring the horn for drinking together,
Full of yearning, tinted, ninth wave's hue,
Long and blue its designs, gold its trim.

. . .

For Moreiddig's hand, sponsor of songs,
Forebears' praise before cold burial.
Marvellous brothers, both high-minded,
Unequal power beneath their brows,
Soldiers who gave to me good service.

. . .

Saviours when needed, red their weapons,
They held their borders against a host.
Praise is their portion, these I speak of—
Keening has come, both taken from me:
Ah Christ ! how grieved am I by the pain
Of Moreiddig's loss, much is he missed.

Owain Cyfeiliog (12th century),
Hirlas Owain,
translated by Joseph P. Clancy.

Some poets believe that poetry is one with *hiraeth* in its mission of recollection of lost states of glory, and prevision of a return to the ideal :

151.

Are the stars above
As splendid and divine as poets sing ?
Their power sublime on our responding spirit,
May it not be the hold of memories dim
Of far diviner scenes, radiant of God ?
The stars are in us ! And all poetry
Is but the recollection of our past,
Or premonition of what we shall be . . .

. . . Our imaginings, who can
Prove or disprove they are the fragments strewn
On a deep sea, the wreck of a nobler life,
And that the soul in stupor lies, until
Recovered by the ever-seeking, living breath
Of poetry ?

Islwyn,
Intimations,
translated by D. M. Lloyd.

As to the effects of the poetry of *hiraeth*, its passionate expression may achieve miracles. :

152. THE LEGEND OF LLYN SAFADDAN

(In olden Wales, it was said that the Birds of Llangorse Lake, Breconshire, knew who was the rightful prince of the district, and would sing for him at his bidding. This story is set in the time of King Henry the Second.)

The winter wind blew thinly in the reeds
Beside Safaddan Lake. Three racing steeds,
Tuned to their riders' mood, grew tensely still,
Trembling like echoes driven from hill to hill.
A vagrant mist came by, and seemed to rest
Where wild fowl crowded on the water's breast.

Then Milo spake. ' My lands and thine, O Payn—
Guarded by mountains, rich with sun and rain !
How good to be a Norman ! ' And he turned
Sharply, and smiling, but with eyes that burned.
' 'Tis mad Welsh Fancy, Gruffydd, makes you hold
These lands are rightly yours ! And since 'tis told
That birds of Lake Safaddan sing to own
Their rightful ruler, and for him alone—
And since you doubt the justice of the King,
I will make trial now, and bid them sing . . .
O Birds of Lake Safaddan, rise and claim
The mighty lord who rules in Henry's name ! '
. . . His ringing challenge rose, and fell, and brake
Where tranquil wings lay mirrored in the lake.

Then Payn dismounted at the water's edge.
' I hold my overlordship as a pledge
To serve the king. Therefore, ye silent throng,
I charge you by his power to raise your song ! '
. . . The echoes jangled in the westering ray
With mockery at themselves, and died away.

So Gruffydd came. He came grave-eyed with truth,
One whose lost heritage had touched his youth,
And by the water-side he knelt in prayer,
As was his wont for battle; and the air
Heard and was still . . . But suddenly he rose
And stretched his arms towards the mountain snows,
The dales, the little rills that laughed in flood—
Land of his fathers, yearning in his blood,
And all the *hiraeth* tembled in his voice,
Bidding the birds arise and sing their choice . . .

Then shook the waters with a rush of wings—
Burst into music as a harp that sings . . .
A mighty sound from wheeling shades and gleams,
Singing with valorous faith, yet soft with dreams,
Voices of a freedom none shall ever break,
Proclaimed for Gruffydd by Safaddan Lake . . .
And shamed usurpers mused upon the wrong
That left a Cymric prince no crown but song.

Melfin Jones

But above all, the poetic expression of *hiraeth*—whether we write, read, or sing it—helps us to make the best of harsh reality, and reconciles us to duty and necessity :

153.

The elder children had crept in from the other room and sat around her in a ring, their white anxious faces raised.

So she sang for them, as she promised, an old Welsh folk song, *Pant Corlan yr Wyn*, about the shearing, and then gave them, as a special treat, a song called *Hen Aelwyd Cymru* (The Old Welsh Hearth), her heart full to brimming. Her breasts had gone out in the flood-tide of her emotion and the old *hiraeth* came up in her throat; her eyes were half shut in the longing, and her beautiful contralto voice, clear and low, went out with an infinite tenderness.

' There now, ' she said at last, as she sent off the elder children to their room. ' That will be three-and-sixpence if you please. Front seats! '

As she tucked up the little one for the night he said, half awake :

' Our Meg . . . ? '

' Hush. '

' You're . . . not going to go away? '

' There's silly! ' she whispered.

' Fine and nice, ' he said, turning over drowsily, the songs still with him.

That was to be her recompense.

Geraint Goodwin,
Saturday Night.

INDEX OF AUTHORS

(The numbers refer to the relevant extracts)

REFERENCES

References are made to the most easily available texts where possible.

1. Welsh Review, III, iv, (1944). (Welsh original in : Hen Benillion, edited by T. H. Parry-Williams, Gwasg Gomer, 1940.)
2. Lawrence Wright Music Co.
3. Marged, T. Glynne Davies, Gwasg Gomer, 1974, pp. 12-13.
4. Hen Benillion, edited by T. H. Parry-Williams, Gwasg Gomer, 1940
5. An Introduction to Welsh Poetry, Gwyn Williams, Faber, 1953, pp. 195-6. (Original Welsh in Ms Mostyn 131, National Library of Wales, Aberystwyth.)
6. Pregethau'r Dr. John Owen, edited by Williams Morris, Llyfrau'r Cyfundeb, 1957.
7. Lowri, Grace Roberts, Brython Press (Hugh Evans & Sons Ltd.), 1958, pp. 194-5.
8. Oriau Eraill, Llyfr V, Hughes a'i Fab, n.d., p. 119.
9. Pigau'r Sêr, J. G. Williams, Gwasg Gee, n.d., pp. 79-80.
10. Penillion Telyn, J. T. Jones, Hughes a'i Fab, n.d., pp. 25-6.
11. Lloyd George: Family Letters, 1885-1936, edited by Kenneth O. Morgan, University of Wales Press and O.U.P., 1973, pp. 97-8.
12. Lowri, Grace Roberts, Brython Press, 1958, pp. 7-8.
13. Beirdd Ein Canrif, I, Gwasg Gomer, 1950, pp. 63-4.
14. Welsh Lyrics of the Nineteenth Century, edited by Edmund O. Jones, J. E. Southall, 1907, p. 70. (Original Welsh in Y Flodeugerdd Gymraeg, edited by W. J. Gruffydd, University of Wales Press, 1936, pp. 17-8).
15. The Works of Sir Lewis Morris, Routledge & Kegan Paul.
16. Gladys of Harlech, or The Sacrifice, Vol. III, Anne Beale, London, 1858, pp. 288-9.
17. Collected Poems, T. Harri Jones, Gwasg Gomer, 1977, p. 129. (Originally in : The Beast at the Door, Rupert Hart-Davis, 1963.)
18. A Bangor Book of Verse, compiled by Sam Jones, Jarvis & Foster, 1924, pp. 17-8.
19. Plasau'r Brenin, D. Gwenallt Jones, Gwasg Aberystwyth, 1934, pp. 116-9.
21. The Land of Wales, Eiluned and Peter Lewis, Batsford, 1937, pp. 110-112.
21. The Penguin Book of Welsh Verse, edited by Anthony Conran, Penguin Books, 1967, p. 127.
22. The Development of Welsh Poetry, H. Idris Bell, O.U.P., 1936, p. 123.
23. The Welsh in America : Letters from Immigrants, Alan Conway, University of Wales Press, 1961, p. 124.
24. A Poet in the Family, Dannie Abse, Hutchinson, 1974, p. 71.
25. The Welsh in America, edited by Alan Conway, University of Wales Press, 1961, p. 124.
26. Poetry of Wales, 1930-1970, edited by R. Gerallt Jones, Gwasg Gomer, 1974, pp. 342-3. (Original Welsh in Mân Gwyn, Christopher Davies, 1965.)
27. The Welsh in America, Alan Conway, University of Wales Press, 1961, p. 35.
28. Welsh People of California: an Historical Sketch Awarded the Prize at San Francisco Eisteddfod, January 1st, 1923, by David Hughes.
29. Wales and the Welsh, Trevor Fishlock, Cassell, 1972, p. 6.
30. Hawkmoor, Lynn Hughes, Christopher Davies, 1977, p. 45. (Also published by Penguin Books, 1977).
31. The Collected Stories of Geraint Goodwin, edited by Sam Adams and Roland Mathias, H. G. Walters, Ltd., 1976, pp. 105-9.
32. O'r Bala i Geneva, Owen M. Edwards, Gwasg y Bala, 1908.
33. An Introduction to Welsh Poetry, Gwyn Williams, Faber, 1953, pp. 218-9.
34. The Anathemata, David Jones, Faber, 1952, pp. 199-200.

35. *The New Oxford Book of English Light Verse*, edited Kingsley Amis, O.U.P., 1978, p. 273.
36. *The Life of Dylan Thomas*, Constantine Fitzgibbon, Dent, 1965, p. 299.
37. *Poems of the Welsh*, H. Idris Bell, The Welsh Printing Co. Ltd., 1913, p. 26.
38. *The Earliest Welsh Poetry*, edited by Joseph P. Clancy, Macmillan, 1970, pp. 43-4. (Original in *Canu Aneurin*, edited by Ifor Williams, University of Wales Press, 1961, p. 15.)
39. *The Poetry of Llywarch Hen*, edited by Patrick K. Ford, University of California, 1974, pp. 40, 69-70, 76-7.
40. *The Earliest Welsh Poetry*, edited by Joseph P. Clancy, Macmillan, 1970, p. 88. (Original in : *Canu Llywarch Hen*, edited by Ifor Williams, University of Wales Press, 1953, p. 51.)
41. *The Lays of Caruth*, Anne Elfe, 1808, reprinted John E. Hardwick, 1909, Newport, Mon., pp. 23-27.
42. *Caneuon Talhaiarn*, Cwmni'r Wasg Genedlaethol Gymreig, Caernarfon, 1902.
43. *Songs of Wales, Book II*, edited Granville Bantock, Paston Music Ltd., n.d., pp. 12-3.
44. *Welsh Grammar* (Prologue), Dr. Gruffydd Robert, University of Wales Press, 1939.
45. *Hen Benillion*, Gwasg Gomer, 1940, p. 124.
46. *Prynu Dol*, Kate Roberts, Gwasg Gee, 1969, pp. 71-79.
47. *O Gors y Bryniau*, Kate Roberts, Hughes a'i Fab, 1925, p. 36-9.
48. *Holl Waith Barddonol Goronwy Owen*, edited by Isaac Foulkes, 1868.
49. *Pregethau'r Dr. John Owen*, edited by William Morris, Llyfrau'r Cyfundeb, 1957.
50. *Ysgrifau*, Dewi Emrys, Hughes a'i Fab, 1937, pp. 14-15.
51. *The Welsh in America*, edited by Alan Conway, University of Wales Press, 1961.
52. *Dial y Tir*, Ambrose Bebb, Gwasg y Brython, 1945, pp. 142-3.
53. *Off to Philadelphia in the Morning*, Jack Jones, Hamish Hamilton, 1947, p. 127.
54. Ditto.p, 138.
55. *Cymru ac America: Wales and America*, David Williams, University of Wales Press, 1975, pp. 85-6.
56. *Definition of a Waterfall*, John Ormond, O.U.P., 1973, p. 42.
57. *The Welsh Colony in Patagonia*, R. Bryn Williams, University of Wales Press, 1965, pp. 15, 43, 71, 73.
58. *Up, Into the Singing Mountain*, Richard Llewellyn, Michael Joseph, 1960, p. 11.
59. *The Anglo-Welsh Review*, No 35, pp. 58-9.
60. *Five Seasons*, Godfrey John, Foursquare Press, Cambridge, Mass., 1977, p. 93.
61. *Poetry Wales*, Vol. 14, No. 3, Winter 1978-9, p. 32.
62. *The Welsh in America*, edited by Alan Conway, University of Wales Press, 1961.
63. Proverb.
64. *A Short History of Wales*, Owen M. Edwards, T. Fisher Unwin, 1906, p. 10.
65. *Cymru ac America: Wales and America*, David Williams, University of Wales Press, 1975, p. 9.
66. *The Strong Man of Australia*, Stanhope W. Sprigg, C. Arthur Pearson, 1916, pp. 12.
67. *Off to Philadelphia in the Morning*, Jack Jones, Hamish Hamilton, 1947,pp. 328-9.
68. *Collected Poems*, T. Harri Jones, Gwasg Gomer, 1977. (Originally in *The Beast at the Door*, Rupert Hart-Davis, 1963, p. 18.)
69. Ditto. (Originally in *The Beast at the Door*, Rupert Hart-Davis, 1963, p. 23).
70. *Hen Benillion*, edited by T. H. Parry-Williams, Gwasg Gomer, 1940.
71. Ditto.
72. *Caneuon Cenedlaethol Cymru : the National Songs of Wales*, edited by E. T. Davies and Sydney Northcote, Boosey & Hawkes, 1959, pp 102-3.
73. *The Burning Tree*, edited by Gwyn Williams, Faber, 1953, pp. 70-1.
74. *The Earliest Welsh Poetry*, edited by Joseph P. Clancy, Macmillan, 1970, pp. 133-4. (Original Welsh in *The Oxford Book of Welsh Verse*, edited by Thomas Parry, O.U.P., 1962, p. 27.)
75. *Hen Benillion*, edited by T. H. Parry-Williams, Gwasg Gomer, 1940, No. 129.
76. *To Look For a Word*, edited by Gwyn Williams, Gwasg Gomer, 1976, p. 121.

77. *Songs of Wales*, edited by A. W. Tomlyn & D. Emlyn Evans, Edinburgh, n.d., p. 46.

78. *Hen Benillion*, edited by T. H. Parry-Williams, Gwasg Gomer, 1940, No. 120.

79. *Caneuon Cenedlaethol Cymru: the National Songs of Wales*, Boosey & Hawkes, 1959, pp. 68-9.

80. *Taliesin* 28, pp. 38-9.

81. *The Burning Tree*, edited by Gwyn Williams, Faber, 1953, pp. 144-7.

82. *The Earliest Welsh Poetry*, edited by Joseph P. Clancy, Macmillan, 1970, p. 184. (Original Welsh in *The Oxford Book of Welsh Verse*, edited by Thomas Parry, O.U.P., 1962, pp. 51-2.)

83. *The Poetry of Llywarch Hen*, edited by Patrick K. Ford, University of California, 1974, p. 68, No. 10.

84. *Poetry of Wales 1930-1970*, edited by R. Gerallt Jones, Gwasg Gomer, 1974, p. 309. (Original Welsh in *Llwybrau'r Pridd*, Christopher Davies, 1961.)

85. *The Journal of The Welsh Folk Song Society*, Vol. II, p. 29, Vol. IV, p. 1, Vol. III, p. 3.

86. *The Burning Tree*, edited by Gwyn Williams, Faber, 1956, pp. 56-7.

87. *Journal of the Welsh Folk Song Society*, Vol. 1, part iv, p. 192.

88. Ditto. Vol. I, part iv, pp. 183-4.

89. *Poetry of Wales 1930-1970*, edited by R. Gerallt Jones, Gwasg Gomer, 1974, pp. 312-3.

90. *A Crown for Branwen*, Harri Webb, Gwasg Gomer, 1974, pp. 48-9.

91. *Ysgrifau*, T. H. Parry-Williams, Foyle's Welsh Department, 1928, pp. 77-80.

92. *Hen Benillion*, edited by T. H. Parry-Williams, Gwasg Gomer, 1940, No. 123.

93. *Caniadau*, Sir John Morris-Jones, Fox Jones & Co., Oxford, 1907, p. 41.

94. *A History of Welsh Literature*, Thomas Parry, translated by H. Idris Bell, O.U.P., 1962, pp. 100-101. (Original in *Gwaith Dafydd ap Gwilym*, edited by Thomas Parry, University of Wales Press, 1963, pp. 46-7.)

95. *Medieval Welsh Lyrics*, edited by Joseph P. Clancy, Macmillan, 1965, pp. 70-71. (Original in *Gwaith Dafydd ap Gwilym*, pp. 276-7.)

96. *Medieval Welsh Lyrics*, edited by Joseph P. Clancy, Macmillan, 1965, pp. 80-82. (Original in *Gwaith Dafydd ap Gwilym*, pp. 204-5.)

97. *Talking of Wales*, Trevor Fishlock, Cassell, 1976, p. 60.

98. *The Oxford Book of Welsh Verse*, edited by Thomas Parry, O.U.P., 1962, p. 530.

99. *Poetry of Wales 1930-1970*, edited by R. Gerallt Jones, Gwasg Gomer, 1974, pp. 200-201. (Original Welsh in *Dail Pren*, Gwasg Aberystwyth, 1965.)

100. *Poetry of Wales 1930-1970*, edited by R. Gerallt Jones, Gwasg Gomer, 1974, pp. 178-9.

101. *Exiles All*, Meic Stephens, Christopher Davies, 1973, pp. 16-17.

102. *Yr Haf a Cherddi Eraill*, R. Willims, Parry, Gwasg y Bala, 1924, p. 44.

104. *Poetry of Wales 1930-1970*, edited by R. Gerallt Jones, Gwasg Gomer, 1974, pp. 154-5. (Original Welsh in *Cerddi'r Daith*, Gwasg Aberystwyth, 1954.)

105. *The Forgotten Country*, Sally Roberts Jones, Gwasg Gomer, 1977, pp. 31-2.

106. *The Penguin Book of Welsh Verse*, edited by Anthony Conran, Penguin Books, 1967, p. 127. (Original Welsh in *Caniadau*, T. Gwynn Jones, Hughes and Son, 1926.)

107. *Poetry of Wales 1930-1970*, edited by R. Gerallt Jones, Gwasg Gomer, 1974, pp. 210-211. (Original Welsh in *Dail Pren*, Gwasg Aberystwyth, 1956.)

108. *The Poetry of the Celtic Races*, Ernest Renan, translated from the French by Williams G. Hutchinson, Walter Scott Ltd., London, 1896, pp. 6-8.

109. *The Works of Matthew Arnold*, Smith Elder, 1867, Vol. V.

110. *The Development of Welsh Poetry*, H. Idris Bell, O.U.P., 1936, pp. 13 ff.

111. *An Introduction to Welsh Poetry*, Gwyn Williams, Faber, 1953, p. 50.

112. *Y Flodeugerdd Gymraeg*, edited by W. J. Gruffydd, University of Wales Press, 1931, pp. 144-5.

113. *Poetry of Wales 1930-1970*, edited by R. Gerallt Jones, Gwasg Gomer, 1974, pp. 390-1. (Original Welsh in *Ysgyrion Gwaed*, Gwasg Gee, 1967.)

114. Proverb.

115. *Poetry of Wales* 1930-1970, edited by R. Gerallt Jones, Gwasg Gomer, 1974, p. 325. (Original Welsh in *Llwybrau'r Pridd*, Christopher Davies, 1961.)
116. *The Flooded Valley*, Roland Mathias, Putman, n.d., p. 23.
117. *Affinities*, Vernon Watkins, Faber, 1962, p. 11.
118. *Bardic Heritage*, edited by Robert Gurney, Chatto & Windus, 1969, pp. 142-3.
119. *Welsh Lyrics of the Nineteenth Century*, edited by Edmund O. Jones, J. E. Southall 1907, pp. 115-6.
120. *Collected Poems*, T. Harri Jones, Gwasg Gomer, 1977. (Originally in *The Colour of Cockcrowing*, Rupert Hart-Davis, 1966, p. 27.)
121. *Collected Poems*, T. Harri Jones, Gwasg Gomer, 1977. (Originally in *The Enemy in the Heart*, Rupert Hart-Davis, 1957, p. 17.)
122. *To Look For a Word*, edited by Gwyn Williams, Gwasg Gomer, 1976, pp. 229-230.
123. *The Poetry of the Celtic Races*, Ernest Renan, translated from the French by William G. Hutchinson, Walter Scott, 1896, p. 25.
124. *To Look For a Word*, edited by Gwyn Williams, Gwasg Gomer, 1976, p.249.
126. *Slings and Arrows: sayings chosen from the speeches of the Rt. Hon. David Lloyd George*, edited by Phillip Guedalla, Cassell, 1929, p. 42.
127. *Buchedd Garmon*, Saunders Lewis, Gwasg Aberystwyth, 1937.
128. *A Sense of Europe*, Raymond Garlick, Gwasg Gomer, 1968, p. 103.
129. *The End of the Vision*, Peter Finch, John Jones Cardiff, 1971, pp. 40-1.
130. *Song at the Year's Turning*, R. S. Thomas, Rupert Hart-Davis, 1960, p. 63.
131. *The Development of Welsh Poetry*, H. Idris Bell, O.U.P., 1936, pp. 13ff.
132. *Plasau'r Brenin*, D. Gwenallt Jones, Gwasg Aberystwyth, 1934, pp. 116-9.
133. *Favourite Welsh and English Hymns and Melodies*, The National Cymanfa Ganu Association of the U.S. and Canada, No. 44.
134. *Y Flodeugerdd Gymraeg*, edited by W. J. Gruffydd, University of Wales Press, 1959, p. 171.
135. *Poetry of Wales* 1930-1970, edited by R. Gerallt Jones, Gwasg Gomer, 1974, p. 134.
136-142 Hymns—see the several denominational hymnbooks.
143. *The Oxford Book of Welsh Verse*, edited by Thomas Parry, O.U.P., 1962, p. 418.
144. *To Look For a Word*, edited by Gwyn Williams, Gwasg Gomer, 1974, pp. 215-6. (Original Welsh in *Y Flodeugerdd Gymraeg*, edited by W. J. Gruffydd, University of Wales Press, 1936, p. 196.)
145. *The Earliest Welsh Poetry*, edited by Joseph P. Clancy, Macmillan, 1970, p. 159.
146. *An Introducion to Welsh Poetry*, Gwyn Williams, Faber, 1953, p. 138. (Original Welsh in *Cywyddau Iolo Goch ac Eraill*, University of Wales Press, 1937, pp. 322-3)
147. *The Oxford Book of English Verse*, edited by A. Quiller-couch, 1939, p. 407.
148. *A Book of Wales*, edited by D. M. and H. M. Lloyd, Collins, 1953, pp. 369-70.
149. *An Introduction to Welsh Poetry*, Gwyn Williams. Faber, 1953, pp. 116-7.
150. *The Earliest Welsh Poetry*, edited by Joseph P. Clancy, Macmillan, 1970, pp. 124-126. (Original Welsh in *The Oxford Book of Welsh Verse*, edited by Thomas Parry, O.U.P., 1962, p. 30.)
151. *A Book of Wales*, edited by D. M. and H. M. Lloyd, Collins, 1953, pp. 369-370.
152. *These Things Remain*, Melfin Jones, Staples Press, 1964, p. 40-1.
153. *Collected Short Stories of Geraint Goodwin*, edited by Sam Adams and Roland Mathias, H. G. Walters, 1976, p. 123.

ACKNOWLEDGEMENTS

Acknowledgements are due to the following for permission to use copyright material :

Granada Publishing Ltd., for poems from *Song at the Year's Turning* by R. S. Thomas, from *The Beast at the Door, The Enemy in the Heart* and *The Colour of Cockcrowing* by T. Harri Jones, and from *These Things Remain* by Melfin Jones ; Michael Joseph Ltd. for an extract from *Up, Into the Singing Mountain* by Richard Llewellyn ; Faber & Faber Ltd. for an extract from *The Anathemata* by David Jones ; Chatto & Windus and the Author's Literary Estate for 'Y Cywydd Diweddaf' from *Bardic Heritage* translated by Robert Gurney ; Anthony Sheil Associates Ltd. for an extract from *A Poet in the Family*, Hutchinson Ltd., © Dannie Abse 1977 ; the Author for extracts from *The Earliest Welsh Poetry* and *Medieval Welsh Lyrics* by Joseph Clancy ; David Higham Associates and the Trustees for the Copyrights of the late Dylan Thomas for a broadcast extract ; Batsford for an extract from *The Land of Wales* by Eiluned and Peter Lewis ; Oxford University Press for extracts from *Definition of a Waterfall* by John Ormond, *The Development of Welsh Poetry* by H. Idris Bell and *A History of Welsh Literature* by Thomas Parry, translated by H. Idris Bell ; Curtis Brown Ltd. and the author for extracts from *The Burning Tree, Presenting Welsh Literature* and *An Introduction to Welsh Poetry* by Gwyn Williams ; poems from *The Poetry of Llywarch Hen* by Patrick K. Ford, © 1974 by the Regents of the University of California, reprinted by permission of the University of California Press ; the poem 'Asking' by Godfrey John first appeared in the *Christian Science Monitor* and subsequently in the Welsh section of the author's collected writings entitled *Five Seasons*. It appears here by permission of Foursquare Press, 4 Merrill Street, Cambridge, MA 02139 U.S.A. ; Cassell Ltd. for extracts from *Wales and the Welsh* and *Talking of Wales* by Trevor Fishlock ; Penguin Books Ltd. for an extract from *The Penguin Book of Welsh Verse* (The Penguin Poets, 1967), p. 127, © Anthony Conran 1967 ; The University of Wales Press for extracts from *The Welsh Colony in Patagonia* by R. Bryn Williams and *Wales and America* by David Williams ; the Univeristy of Minnesota Press for extracts from *The Welsh in America : letters from the immigrants* edited by Alan Conway, © 1961 by the University of Minnesota ; the National Library of Wales for an extract from *Lloyd George : Family Letters* 1885-1936, edited by Kenneth O. Morgan ; Gee & Son (Denbigh) Ltd. for extracts from *Pigau'r Sêr* by J. G. Williams and *Prynu Dol* by Kate Roberts ; Christopher Davies Ltd. for poems from *Llwybrau'r Pridd* by T. Glynne Davies and *Man Gwyn* by Bobi Jones ; Hughes a'i Fab for extracts from *Ysgrifau* by Dewi Emrys and *O Gors y Bryniau* by Kate